"So, how was your date with Mac?"

Rich's voice was nonchalant as he faced Beth across the lunch table.

"With Mac?" Beth almost gave the game away. She had spent the evening with her Multiple Access Computer. "Oh, MAC and I—we had a wonderful time. We went to a cozy place and we—talked back and forth—Lord, until past midnight. We're so looking forward to June."

"I don't want to hear about that," he snapped.

"Well, you showed an interest. I was even going to invite you to the wedding!" She clapped her hand over her mouth, realizing she had gone too far.

Look at him glare. He thinks I'm inviting him to my wedding, and when he finds out the invitation is to his wedding, he'll really blow his stack!

Emma Goldrick describes herself as a grandmother first and an author second. She was born and raised in Puerto Rico where she met her husband, a career military man from Massachusetts. His postings took them all over the world, which often led to mishaps—such as the Christmas they arrived in Germany before their furniture. Emma uses the places she's been as backgrounds for her books, but just in case she runs short of settings, this prolific author and her husband are always making new travel plans.

Books by Emma Goldrick

Temporary Paragon

Emma Goldrick

Harlequin Books

TORONTO • NEW YORK • LONDON
AMSTERDAM • PARIS • SYDNEY • HAMBURG
STOCKHOLM • ATHENS • TOKYO • MILAN

by Mills & Boon Limited

ISBN 0-373-02889-X

Harlequin Romance first edition February 1988

CHAPTER ONE

BETH MURPHY barely managed to stagger up the front steps of the old wooden three-decker in South Boston, identical to all its neighbours, and dropped into a chair. Three of the biggest boys on her Little League baseball team clattered their spikes behind her, depositing the duffel bags full of bats and paraphernalia in odd corners. She waved them off, and they tramped out of the house, not at all unhappy.

'Good God, Beth, you look a mess. What the devil is an unmarried——'

'Spinster,' Beth interrupted, in her husky voice.

'I wasn't going to say that.'

'But I did, Mary. It's true, I admit it—in fact, I'm proud of it. And I do it because they couldn't find a manager for the team, and the kids wouldn't have been able to play baseball in the league if I didn't volunteer!'

'So there!' Mary Lockridge laughed, rolling her wheelchair away from the desk. She was a tiny, dark-haired woman, daughter of an old Italian family from the North End, who had married a warm-hearted Old Yankee, and come to South Boston to settle. Despite the leg problems that had bothered her since birth, she managed well in a wheelchair, adequately on crutches, and from time to time essayed 'unsupported flight', as she called it. And she was an office manager *par excellence*.

Beth tugged the old baseball cap off her head. Her mass of golden-red hair fell down to her shoulders. She shook her head a couple of times to free the tangles. 'Got a Coke?' she asked.

'Not exactly,' Mary chuckled. 'I've got a tiger by the tail here, though.' She gestured towards the telephone handset lying on her desk. 'Mr Pomp and Circumstance himself. Wants to talk to the Manager. There may be a Seven-Up left in the fridge there. How was the game?'

Beth stretched up to her slender five foot six and stalked the fridge. 'I think we had a moral victory,' she gloated as she pulled a bottle of pop out of the ice. 'The last time we played this team they beat us twenty-five to nothing. This time they only won by seven to one. That's our—where the heck is the bottle-opener?'

'On the desk, silly. Where I always keep it.'

'You're going to die of neatness, Mary. Why are you leaving the tiger hanging on the telephone?'

'He thinks I'm running around looking for the Manager. You were saying?'

'I was saying, gloating, that's the first run we've scored all year!' The telephone made squawking noises. 'You really want me to talk to him?'

'Not particularly,' Mary laughed. 'But if you want to, I don't mind. It's a quarter to five, and I've had enough for this week. Thank God it's Friday!'

'Amen.' Beth walked slowly over to the desk and picked up the telephone. 'Good day, this is Miss Murphy speaking.'

'This is the manager of Rentasec? Just a minute for Mr Macomber, please.' Beth shook her head, laughing. The old one-upmanship business. I won't put my boss on the line until yours is on. It was a game played in every business, but Beth was not at all impressed.

'Hello.' A male growl, low-pitched, indignant. Oh lord, here's one who not only got up on the wrong side of the bed, but stayed there all day! she thought. 'It's about time,' he continued. 'I've been waiting for almost eight minutes.'

Another one of those, Beth groaned to herself. She was just not in the mood for playing the game. 'Well, we can't all jump at command,' she said. 'There are other things that require doing.' And I hope that's cold enough for you, Mr Macomber.

'Not when you're dealing with me,' the voice returned. 'When I call, I get instant action.'

'Do you really?' she sighed, and then, in pseudo-sympathy, 'You must have a terrible kidney problem in your organisation.'

There was a second of silence, followed by a gruff laugh. 'OK, so you put me in my place. I'll just have to chalk that up on my board. Now, where was I?'

'Rentasec,' she prompted, trying to hide the giggle.

'Rentasec. Yes. I've been told you keep a staff of qualified executive secretaries.'

'That's correct. For temporary work, of course.'

'Tell me about it.' It was a command, not an invitation. Beth shrugged at Mary, and motioned her to go ahead closing up the office.

'Rentasec is a co-operative association of sixty women who have retired from the business scene to raise families,' she explained. 'Forty of our members are highly skilled, and we provide updating briefings regularly.'

'You've got a sexy voice, lady. What do the other twenty do?'

Startled, Beth half lowered the receiver, covered the mouthpiece, and called to Mary, 'Who is this Macomber?'

'He's the Chief Operating Officer of Macomber Publishers,' she was told in one ear.

'Well——?' the telephone barked at her. Beth shook her head to clear her mind. The game must have been a greater strain than she had thought.

'I——' She fumbled for a moment, then pulled her well known reserve around her like a suit of armour. 'The remaining members act as baby-sitters while our front-line people are at work,' she said as coldly as she could.

She must have been successful. 'Brrrrr,' he chuckled. 'Mighty cold in Boston these days, isn't it?' Beth was not about to answer. 'Well, I need an executive secretary,' he added. 'Somebody who understands word processing and computer techniques. Someone old enough not to giggle every time I say something. Someone who's not husband-hunting.'

'I think all of our personnel qualify,' she said stiffly. 'We deal only in the best.'

'Oh, and somebody who knows how to handle people, big and little ones,' he added. 'What are you doing tonight?'

Thrown off-track again, Beth sputtered, then settled down. 'Isn't that rather personal, Mr Macomber?'

'Of course,' he returned. 'We're talking about my own executive secretary. It's bound to be a personal relationship.'

'I'm sure it must be,' she said frigidly, having made up her mind. 'As for myself, I intend to spend the weekend with MAC.' She looked fondly into the next room, crammed with racks that made up their Multiple Access Computer.

'Lucky guy,' he said. His voice had shifted from harshness into a smooth baritone, an almost *come-hither* sound. It was time to turn him off.

'Unfortunately, Mr Macomber,' she said politely, 'a firm like ours must be most selective of our clients. We couldn't possibly send our ladies out in an environment where a concubine is wanted. We deal only with secretaries.'

'Well, I'll be damned——'

'Probably,' she sighed, and dropped the handset on to its cradle.

'What was that all about?' Mary wheeled herself back from the computer room, a smile teasing her olive-toned Italian skin.

'I'm darned if I know,' Beth said reflectively. She thought it over for a minute. 'I don't know just what the man really wanted—but I turned the job down, anyway. Macomber. Publishing? Probably some old fogey in his third childhood, I'll bet. He wants a temporary secretary who's willing to play footsy with him. What the devil are you laughing at now?'

'Take a look at this.' Mary held out a page from the *Globe*. 'The Governor's ball. See the man next to him?'

The Governor of Massachusetts was short and slim. Next to him was a lean, hawk-eyed six-footer. The black and white picture failed to do him justice. 'Brown hair, brown eyes—curly eyelashes,' Mary giggled. 'Ramrod Macomber, they called him in his college days. He's the playboy of the year in Boston, Beth. Where've you been lately? His publishing company handles the hottest detective stories in the country—and a mess of those "take off all your clothes" books—historical romances.'

'Hysterical romances, you mean? My, he certainly might be able to catch someone—especially in a small office. Curly eyelashes? Isn't that a shame? Well, I turned him down, anyway. He probably needs someone from the Combat Zone, not Rentasec.'

'Not to worry,' Mary told her, handing over a computer sheet. 'Most of our girls are committed for next week, anyway. I never cease thanking God for this computer. The next time your brother comes in from California, I'm going to kiss him—homely as he is.' She wheeled her chair over to the terminal, and punched a few more keys. The big machine in the next room grumbled, flashed a few lights, and settled down to its weekend run of mundane things. Payrolls, government-required statistics, postings of earnings, that sort of thing.

'Fred really did a good job of programming,' Beth agreed. 'And spent his four-week vacation rustling up the parts cheaply—that was a sacrifice, too.'

'It used to be a girl's best friend was a diamond,' Mary chortled. 'Now it's a brother who's a computer-magician.'

'We could have scored twice,' muttered Beth, her mind already back to the baseball game. 'Would you believe it—Robbie Bettencourt hasn't had a hit all season. They walked him. He was so proud he tried to steal second base, their catcher threw the ball out into the outfield, and Robbie walked home!'

'Sounds like an average Little League day to me,' Mary laughed. 'Lucky you turned the man down. MAC says we don't have an executive secretary free on Monday.'

'Oh, wow,' Beth sighed. 'Sixty members in our co-operative, and we haven't a one free for Monday?'

'Hey, well, thirty-five of them are on assignment, fifteen are baby-sitting for the working mothers, and the others have various ailments and aches. We grow old, Beth.'

'Don't *say* that,' Beth laughed. 'I don't mind being a spinster, but I *don't* grow old. Why don't you scoot home, love?'

'I will, Beth. Spending the weekend alone again?'

'I suppose. With MAC, as I told the gentleman

on the telephone. There are a number of things to clear up.'

'You know what you need, Beth?'

'Yeah. A good right-handed pitcher. Surely there's some kid in the area who can throw the ball all the way from the pitcher's mound to home-plate?'

'That isn't what I was thinking. What you need is a man!'

'Yeah, one who's four foot three and can throw a good high inside pitch,' Beth chuckled. 'Go on, now. Your husband will be frothing at the bit.'

'No, he won't. I cook better than that.'

The two of them walked each other to the back door, where ramps had displaced stairs long ago. Beth stood at the door as Mary navigated the slope and headed next door to her own house.

Beth stopped for a minute on the back porch. The house, designed exactly like all ten of the neighbours, was a huge three-storey affair, originally cold-water tenements built at the turn of the century. But they were built for large families, and were built well. Each floor contained eight rooms, with a double sitting-room separated by sliding doors. Plumbing had been improved, and in most of the houses on the street, each tenement had been broken up into flats. But not Beth's pride. The house had been left to her by her father. She lived in the expansive second-floor apartment, devoted the first floor to her business, and rented out the third. Housing was tight in Boston. The three-decker that sold for thirty thousand dollars three years ago was now quoted at one hundred and twenty thousand, and there were few houses offered for sale. Meanwhile, the rental income from the third floor paid the taxes, and there was no mortgage. She leaned back against one of the porch pillars and took a deep breath.

The wind was in the right direction for deep

breathing, a flock of sparrows were conducting flight manoeuvres over her tiny back yard, and Beth Murphy's world seemed altogether satisfactory. She had spent all of her life here in the district, within walking distance of Telegraph Hill, and was at peace with herself.

She started to make the rounds of the office area, checking windows, locking doors, and setting the alarm system. It had been a long time ago since one could leave unlocked doors in Southie. Climbing the steep back-stairs brought protests from her knees. She smiled, revealing the two dimples, one on either side of her heart-shaped face, the bane of her existence. Without them, she looked her age. The dimples cut her back almost to sweet sixteen, a time she hardly cared to remember.

Not because I was somebody at sweet sixteen, she told herself as she laboured up the stairs, but because I was a red-headed freckle-faced nobody, who knew nothing. She unlocked the door at the second landing and went in, laughing. Mrs Hennessey, who obliged with cleaning three days a week, was giving the kitchen a last swipe with her dusty cloth.

'Something funny?' The stooped little old lady must have been seventy if she was a day, but had no intention of stopping work 'until the day they pat me in the face with a shovel', she would say from time to time.

'Just reminiscing,' shrugged Beth. 'You're not done yet? It's pretty late.'

'Ain't nothing to go home to,' her housekeeper returned. 'Tell me what's funny and I'll make you a cup of coffee.'

'It wasn't much, but you're on. I could use some coffee.' And *she* could use someone to listen to, Beth thought, as she pulled an old wooden chair out from the kitchen table and sat down. The coffee was hot, and percolated, evidence of premeditation. Weekends were lonely times for the elderly. Having outlived all their friends and families, they turned to anyone who would listen. Beth took a grateful sip.

'Well, I was thinking, coming up the stairs, about being sixteen and red-headed and freckled, and stupid—and it struck me that only the *freckled* part has changed. How about that?'

'Not red-headed, either,' the old lady told her. 'In the summer, when you're out in the sun, it's more gold than red. You remind me of your grandmother. Now, there was a one.'

'Sweet and demure?' Beth knew the answer, but was encouraging the tale.

'A real hell-raiser,' Mrs Hennessy chuckled. 'Me and your grandma, we cut many a swing in our younger days.'

Beth settled back to listen with one ear. The story improved on each telling, this tale of the Irish in South Boston before the Great War, but a good listener knew where to grunt, or comment, or giggle, without even listening. And it gave time to assess the week. Business had been good. Baseball had been terrible. And to end up with some institutional grouch like Ramrod Macomber—wow, there was a name!

The housekeeper had come to the end of her weekly tale, and was ready to leave. Beth said all the right words, paid her for the week, and watched her out of the door with her usual warnings. 'And watch those stairs. I'll see you Monday!'

'Time to unwind,' Beth told herself when the door was safely closed. She added just a dollop of Irish Mist to her coffee, and took it along with her to the bathroom. The tub was old: six feet of white enamel set up on four clawed feet, with a shower-head added years later. Casually, she dropped off her clothes a

piece at a time, leaving a scattered trail between the
living-room and the bathroom, and turned on the
hot-water tap. The heater was in the cellar, requiring
a long run of cold before the warm water arrived.
She waited until the temperature met her needs,
turned on the cold water to balance, and pulled the
shower curtain around the tub.

It was a long step upward to get in. She managed,
revelled in the water, then lathered up with her
favourite perfumed soap. There had been more brick-
dust at the park than she needed, and half of it had
come home in her hair, so she shampooed vigor-
ously, and then just stood there, letting the
comforting warmth run down off her shoulders,
across her small, pert breasts, and down her stomach.
The soap was barely out of her hair when she heard
the noise in the kitchen.

'Stupid,' she chided herself. 'You didn't lock the
back door!'

Leaving the shower water running, she fumbled
her way out of the tub, slipping on the loose bathmat.
Her ancient robe hung on the back of the door. She
shrugged herself into it, still wet, with soap on her
cheeks and ears. There was no weapon in sight
except for the rubber-tipped plunger. She hefted it.
It would have to do. She eased the bathroom door
open and peeped out. There was nobody in the
living-room, but the noises persisted from the kitchen.
Holding her plunger up with two hands, she crept
across the room, leaving a trail of wet footprints on
the old carpet.

Somebody was in the kitchen, crying. Call the
police, her subconscious dictated. Run like hell, her
careful mind admonished. Ignoring them both, she
eased herself around the corner of the door, and
into the kitchen. Somebody was sitting at the table,

head down on her arms. All that was visible was the bright blonde head of hair.

'Stacy?' she asked, disbelievingly. The young head snapped up, tears still coursing.

'Aunt Beth!' The girl scraped back her chair and came running around the table into her aunt's arms. 'Oh God, Aunt Beth, I had to come!'

And that's par for the course, Beth told herself as she welcomed the tiny creature to her side. Anastasia Murphy, eighteen years old, five foot two, platinum blonde, full figure, empty head. The daughter of her brilliant brother Fred, who, at this very moment, ought to be happily ensconced in her dormitory at Marymont College, in upper New York State.

'Hey, you're always welcome,' she whispered softly into the silky crown of hair. 'That's what aunts are for.'

'Oh God, Aunt Beth. I'm in terrible trouble!'

Beth squeezed the girl a little tighter, her chin firming up. 'There's a man involved?' she asked softly.

'Oh—yes. How did you know?'

Beth smiled gently and patted the girl's head. In a typical Irish family, when a girl got herself into 'terrible trouble', it meant only one thing. But first, somehow, she had to stem the hysteria.

'Everything will be all right,' she soothed. 'You'll stay a while. I'll let your father know——'

'Oh—no, not that. Don't let him know!'

'But he'll worry about you, Stacy. We'll tell him that there's a break in the college schedule, and you—decided to take pity on your poor old aunt. How about that for a solution?'

The blonde head at her breast nodded up and down, and it *did* seem that the tears were slowing. With the skill of long practice, Beth manoeuvred the girl back into a chair. Her three brothers had already provided her with seven nieces—none of whom thought it at all unusual to run to their Aunt Beth. 'There now, I was about to make supper, and——'

'It was terrible. Lord, it's good to be here! Everything is so—so ordinary.'

How about that for your obituary? Beth fumed to herself as she headed back to the bathroom to dry off and dress. *Everything about Aunt Beth is so ordinary!* I have three brilliant brothers, each in their own field, but the *daughter of the house* is ordinary!

She was standing in the middle of the bathroom, without a stitch to her name, running the hot air into her hair, and caught a glimpse of herself in the mirror. Luckily, the mirror's cracked, she told herself, as she assessed. Tall enough—for a girl. Nice hair, when it dries—if only it didn't curl so impetuously at its ends. Green eyes that sparkled, stormed, smiled, at need. Square shoulders, with two freckles left from childhood, right in the hollow. Breasts that stood out firmly but not boastfully, tipped bronze, sometimes aching. A flat stomach that narrowed precipitously before it swelled out into ample hips. Legs, perhaps too long for the rest of her, gracefully shaped. Not at all bad for an ordinary old hag, she assured herself. And then, not giving herself a chance to change her mind, she rushed out through the living-room into her bedroom, and dressed.

How did you welcome a niece in trouble? By casual dress, for one thing. It was still cool in the Maytime evening of Boston, and the radiator heat was inefficient. She shrugged herself into a cashmere pullover, stepped into the tiny briefs that were always so at odds with her personality, and snatched up a wrap-around plaid skirt. Her hair fell into place with a simple brushing, and she was ready to act as the family crying-towel.

Stacy had found herself a cigarette, still sitting at

the table. 'Hey, you're in *my* house now.' The girl guiltily stubbed out the butt in her empty coffee-cup.

'I forgot,' Stacy apologised. 'I was feeling—nervous, and I thought a cigarette would——'

'Put you ten steps closer to lung cancer,' her aunt chided. 'Have you been travelling long?'

'A—friend—brought me all the way by car,' the girl said, and ducked her head out of Beth's line of vision. 'About eight hours. It's a nice car.'

'I'll bet. College boy?'

'Oh, heavens, no! An adult. I don't go out with college boys. They're so—so young.'

'Of course,' Beth sighed. I don't go out with college boys either, she thought. Of course, I *did* walk by Harvard yard one time, and look through the gates!

'What are you thinking about, Beth?'

She smiled back at her niece as she opened the refrigerator door and assessed her stock of food. 'Oh, nothing important. Just what a nice time youth was. Will steak do for your supper?'

'Oh yes, fine. I'm hungry. The dining-room at college is—not very good. And Dad sends me such a small allowance.'

'Yes, of course. There's a head of lettuce there. Want to make us a tossed salad? I must say that dress looks good on you. I thought most college kids—er—students, wore jeans.'

'Yes, usually. You like it?' The girl twirled around. Her crimson skirt flared and followed her. 'I changed at North Station. I—well——'

'Putting your best foot forward for your aunt?' Beth laughed.

The girl blushed and confessed, 'Yes. Dad always coached us before we came to your house. "Get dressed like a woman—your aunt doesn't like unisex nieces".'

They worked side by side, the effort easing the tension. When everything was prepared, and the steaks were grilling, Beth hugged the girl again. 'Why don't you get a quick shower or bath?' she suggested. 'And remember to turn on the hot water first, or you're liable to get scalded.'

Beth waited outside the bathroom door until she heard the shower running, and then dashed through to the telephone and dialled her brother's office in California. The time difference came out just right. It was almost six o'clock in Boston, and coffee-break time in Palo Alto.

'It's Beth,' she hissed into the receiver. 'I have your errant daughter here.'

'Well, that's a damn relief,' said Fred. 'The Dean called her mother two hours ago, with some crazy mixed-up message. I might have known she'd go to you. What's the trouble?'

'I don't know, Fred. Don't worry about her. I'll find out, and do something.'

'Well, I'll worry, anyway,' he chuckled. 'I know you mean well, Beth, but you being the baby of the family, I worry about you, too.'

'Well, you needn't,' she told him huffily. 'I've managed to get along without all you men for some time now!'

'That's what worries me,' her brother returned. 'Seen any good ball-games lately?'

'No. Why did you have to ask me that? The Red Sox are in last place in the American League. And so is my Little League team. You couldn't find me a pitcher, I don't suppose?'

'Right after you straighten my daughter out and get her back to college.'

'Well—er—that might take some doing, Fred. I think we have *big* problems.'

'And there's nobody in the family better at settling *big* problems than you,' he laughed. 'I worry about the little ones, but with big ones you're some sort of marvel. How's the computer coming along?'

'Doing fine, Fred. I have to run. Stacy's almost finished with the shower, and——'

'And she told you not to call her old man, I suppose?'

'I suppose,' Beth sighed. 'Funny, how you understand her so well, and yet she continually gets in trouble.'

'That's why we named her Anastasia Elizabeth,' Fred chuckled, and hung up.

'Is that somebody on the telephone for me?' Stacy came hurrying out of the bathroom, looking like some sort of angel, wearing Beth's best robe.

'No. Just a neighbour. Are you expecting a call?'

'Well, I—I thought he might call.'

'He? Does someone else know that you're in Boston?'

'I—I suppose they must. I hope the steak isn't burning.'

And so do I, Beth told herself wryly. Young she might be, but my lovely little niece surely knows how to change the subject!

Supper was a little strained. Stacy was so obviously trying to avoid a whole range of subjects that conversation was like walking through a minefield. They talked about the weather in Boston, the weather in Buffalo, the spring fashion styles, and family anecdotes. But no matter how often Beth pressed the girl about her life at the college, she clammed up and went on to something else.

It was almost ten o'clock that night, over coffee, that she managed to get an indication of the size of the problem. 'You might as well stop dodging the issue, Stacy,' she said. 'We've just got to take the bull by the horns. Are there any other clichés that fit? I suppose this is all about a boy?'

'Well—not exactly a boy. Roddy is a very grown-up man.'

Stacy's coffee-cup was rattling in its saucer as she ducked away from her aunt's eyes.

'Roddy? That's an unusual name. Is he someone from the college?'

'Well—no. Not from Marymont. He's somewhat —older. He was a graduate student at Cornell, and he came over to—I—he just happened to—drop in. He wanted to consult with one of our instructors, and he and I—we just happened to run into each other on the campus.'

'I'll just bet you did, love. Come on, tell all.'

'Well, it took considerable doing,' the girl said indignantly. 'I had to wait the longest time for him to come around the corner and knock me over. It wasn't easy.'

'I'll just bet it wasn't. And does our Roddy have a last name?'

'I—that's the trouble, Aunt Beth. He's *not* our Roddy. He just—he just doesn't care. Not a bit.'

'Doesn't care? You mean, you explained everything to him?'

'Yes. The day after he—after we—I tried to explain it all, and he said it was just not possible, because we had only done it once, you know, and—he—left.'

'Just like that, he left?'

'Well, he stopped long enough to say goodbye and he left. I think he was scared, or something.'

'That's a fine thing! He darned well ought to be. But you came up to Boston with him?'

'Not exactly. With one of his friends.'

'So that means there are at least three of you who know about all this,' Beth snapped. 'You didn't tell me the last name of this paragon of yours.'

'I—his name is—Macomber.'

'Macomber? Roddy Macomber?'

The girl's head snapped up. 'You know him?'

'Ramrod Macomber! No, I don't know him, darling, but I'm *going* to!'

'Ramrod? I've never heard him called that.'

'Well, they do occasionally, I'm told. He's a man who obviously needs taking down a peg or two.'

'Aunt Beth,' the girl said anxiously. 'I don't want him taken down any pegs. I just want to——' The tears began again.

'Are you in love with him?'

'Yes—I—I want to marry him, and—oh God, Aunt Beth, what a mess I've made!'

'Nothing's impossible,' sighed Beth as she tried to soothe away the tears again. 'Why don't you go to bed and rest those tired eyes. Aunt Beth will take care of it, believe me!'

CHAPTER TWO

BETH knew just what she wanted to do on Monday morning, but had no idea how to go about it. She wandered around the empty office, warming up the computer, casually checking the tape-drivers. Stacy was still asleep upstairs, and might well be at it until noon or later. Mary wheeled herself in at nine o' clock, surprised to find the doors already unlocked.

'Forgotten something?' she aked cheerfully.

'Probably,' Beth returned glumly. 'I'm so badly off that I've even forgotten what I might have forgotten.'

'That's a terrible pun, Beth. Good Lord, who could be calling at *this* hour of the morning?'

'I don't know. Why don't you pick up the phone and find out?

'Why don't you?'

'I—I'm sorry, Mary. There isn't any reason why I shouldn't, is there?' So she did, feeling the weight of a guilty conscience prodding at her.

'Rentasec?' That deep male voice—unforgettable. Gruff, but not overbearing.

'Yes. This is Miss Murphy. How may I help you?'

'Miss Murphy—damn it, surely you have a first name?'

'I surely do. How may we help you?'

'Like that, huh?'

Beth sighed. 'I'm really not at my best on Monday mornings, Mr Macomber. It *is* Mr Macomber, isn't it?'

'Yes. You knew damn well who it was. What

22

other sorehead do you have on your lists?'

'Well, we have a number of them, actually,' she said briskly. 'But I wouldn't include you. You're not on our list.'

'And that's what I called you about,' he grumbled. 'look, Miss Murphy, I'm desperate. The whole business is likely to come to a standstill. I don't know how to make these stupid machines go!'

'I'm sure you have a dozen secretaries in the building who do, Mr Macomber. Why don't you try one of them?'

'What the hell do—I mean—pardon me—I've done that.' The voice had shifted up-register to the smooth-as-silk approach. 'I've really tried all the members of our organisation, from editors down to assistant typists.'

'And none of them can make things go? What's the name of your program, Mr Macomber?'

'Richard. My friends call me Richard. Wait a minute.' There was a hum of voices off-telephone, and then he came back. 'The program is called Supergram. Are you familiar with that?'

Beth covered the mouthpiece of the telephone with one hand. 'Supergram, Mary,' she called.

Her office manager smiled, keyed the computer, and compared. 'The same program as ours,' she called back. 'Different name. A few different lock-words, that sort of thing.'

'Mr Macomber? As it happens, we have someone available who is familiar with that program. You realise, of course, there will be an extra fee. Specialisation costs.'

'Damn it, I don't care. How soon can you get her over here to Liberty Square?'

'Well—there's the matter of—it's some distance. Perhaps by one o' clock?'

'Have her take a cab, for God's sake. Make it

ten-thirty!' And he hung up with a mighty crash.

'I take it we're dealing with Macomber Publishing?' Mary asked.

'Indeed we are.'

'But we haven't anyone available, Beth.'

'Yes, we do, Mary. I'm going on this one myself!'

'After what you said on Friday?'

'After what I heard on Saturday. I have a bone to pick with this man. You'd better expect me to be gone for a while. And Stacy is upstairs.'

'That empty-headed minx?' exclaimed Mary.

'The very one. She needs to be kept busy. Dig up something around the office for her to work at.'

'What is this—a therapy course?'

'More likely the devil and idle hands,' said Beth. 'I've got to go change. Liberty Square. Call me a cab, Mary, while I go up and dress for the occasion.'

She hadn't a great deal to choose from. Beth spent little time in society—even the neighbourhood society. As a result, her wardrobe was designed strictly for office work or baseball. But she chose her clothing as a knight might choose his armour—to fit the battle in front of her. So she ended up in a navy-blue skirt, with matching blazer, and a simple white blouse stippled with lace at the collar, down the line of buttons in front, and at the cuffs.

She scrubbed her face carefully, put on a thin layer of moisturiser, and brushed her hair tightly back to the nape of her neck, fastening it there into a chignon.

'Liberty Square,' she told the cab driver. 'And don't hurry.'

The office building was actually on Broad Street, about a block from the square. An unpretentious building, it seemed dwarfed among its neighbours of the Financial District. A discreet brass sign beside the main door said 'Macomber Press'. And a harried elderly man was standing inside, waiting.

'From Rentasec?' he asked anxiously. She offered him a smile. Macomber was her target, not his minions. The thought brought laughter. She had waited for years for a chance to use that word, and had never succeeded until now.

'Brent—Personnel,' he introduced himself, trying out a very dry chuckle, as if hoping her laughter meant good news for a change.

'Murphy—Rentasec,' said Beth as solemnly as she could, while extending a hand. 'I understand you have a set of machines that won't behave? Lead me to the culprits.' He heaved a sigh of relief, and gestured in the direction of a tiny box-elevator. The machine lurched slowly upwards, with not another word exchanged. My dragon really does have his troops under his thumb, she thought. Look at this one. You'd think his life was in danger!

The elevator rumbled to a halt on the fourth floor, fumbled to adjust itself to floor level, and then opened its doors with a hiss, almost as if the machinery was not quite sure it had made it. A long, deserted hall stretched before her. There was not a sound to be heard. She shifted her bag to her other shoulder and followed Brent down the hall, stealing a glance into each of the cubicles as she went. They were all filled with people, sitting at desks in front of computer terminals—and not moving a muscle.

'In here.' The personnel man opened an office door for her, but did not come in. She turned back to look at him. He gestured straight ahead, where an inner office beckoned. She shrugged her shoulders at him, and looked around the office where she stood.

A wide secretarial desk, cluttered with papers, filled the corner under the windows, which surprised her. Most secretaries in big businesses got fluorescent

lights, not windows. To one side of the desk a
terminal sat, muttering to itself. A line of filing
cabinets filled the other walls. And a small vase,
with a single rosebud, stood in the middle of the
desk. 'Welcome to Oz,' she told herself, consulting
her watch. It was only ten twenty-five. She went
around behind the desk, tried out the luxurious
swivel-chair, tested a drawer or two in the desk, and
quietly folded her hands. At exactly ten-thirty she
stood up, brushed down her skirt, rearranged her
blazer, and started for the inner door.

'Isn't she here yet?' The same gruff voice from the
telephone connection, but louder. She stepped across
the threshold, almost losing herself in the thick rug.
The office was fairly large, with a mahogany table
instead of a desk, a little conversation nook set in
the corner, and one very large man, standing with
his back to her, looking out at the pigeons dive-
bombing the street.

'Well—is she here?'

'I believe she is,' Beth answered in her low, husky
voice. He whirled around, the open tails of his light
jacket swinging after him.

'Good Lord!' he exclaimed.

'Good Lord!' she said simultaneously. The man
facing her looked as if he had been run over by a
beer-truck. The left side of his face was covered by
a patch-bandage. His nose was covered with another,
smaller, bandage. A series of scratches filled up his
right cheek and, above all the pristine whiteness, his
dark eyes glared at her.

'You first,' he growled.

'They really *are* curly,' she gasped.

'What?'

'Your eyelashes. Somebody told me they curled.
And they really do!'

He grunted something, and his mouth opened on

a perfect set of gleaming white teeth. 'Is that all you have to say?'

'Well, that's all I can see,' she said tensely. 'Can I believe you are Mr Macomber?'

'You can believe it,' he sighed, moving over to his executive chair and slumping into it.'

'I'd love to see the other guy,' she offered.

'Other guy?'

'Well, there was a fight, wasn't there?'

Those lovely teeth grinned at her again. 'A woman of wit,' he commented.

'Well, you're half right,' she replied automatically. It was one of her father's favourite puns. 'I'm Murphy.'

'Murphy?' He looked up at her. 'You mean, you're the one I talked to on the phone?' She nodded. He waved towards a chair. 'Sit down, Murphy. Come to do the job yourself, or just looking us over before trusting us with one of your little helpers?'

'Probably a little of both,' she said pertly, perching herself on the forward edge of the nearest chair. He stared at her. She was dressed most demurely. If a man could neglect the handsome bulge of breast that stretched the blouse, or pay no attention to the graceful legs that stretched out beneath the knee-length skirt. Or the riot of red-gold hair that was already escaping from its confinement. And this man couldn't.

'You don't look old enough to be manager of a company,' he said, challenging her. 'We never did settle what your first name is.'

'If it makes your day, you *do*,' she returned.

'Do what?'

'Look old enough to be president of a company —two companies. And if you don't care to call me Murphy, you can call me Miss Murphy.'

'I see.'

It was almost impossible to tell what he was thinking. He was giving a good imitation of a mummy. Under the circumstances she fell back on the old Irish tradition of wise-cracking in a tight spot.

'Might I ask what happened?'

'Automobile accident,' he reported. 'My secretary and I were driving back from Cornell——'

'Ah—Cornell!' Bingo, Beth told herself. The target is confirmed!

'You know Cornell?'

'I know *about* it. What happened? You hit a truck or something?'

'My secretary was driving. *She* hit a truck or something, and almost went through the windscreen. She hadn't fastened her seat-belt.'

'Oh, heavens!' Any sign of people-problems brought Beth's sympathy into action, even for a woman she had never met. 'Is she—badly injured?'

'Not critically,' he returned, leaning forward. 'Why would you care?'

'Because she's a person,' Beth snapped indignantly. 'She deserves dignity and sympathy. I don't suppose you ever thought of her that way?'

'Miss Murphy, I think we're getting off the subject, aren't we?'

Her face flushed. She struggled to tamp down her anger. She already knew what he had done to her niece; he probably also kicked dogs and stole ice-cream from little children! But to trap a monster like this one, first you have to examine the surroundings, right?

'Yes, well——' She struggled a little further and managed to produce a very weak smile. 'I don't understand what a publishing company is doing up to its—er—bindery in computers, Mr Macomber.'

'Nor do I,' he admitted ruefully. 'It's an old family firm, run by my father. As best I can remember when I used to look around, everybody had a pencil and a harried look. But my father got himself swept up in the world of the future, and converted everything to electrons. Our authors send in little disks instead of manuscripts, our editors poke around with keyboards instead of red pencils, and everything but the coffee-pot seems to be wired to the machine.'

'And today you can't make it function?'

'That seems to be our problem. Grace comes in early every morning, does something to her terminal, and that releases all the others in the building. It's a security system, or something like that. Does it make sense to you?'

'Not exactly. So what do you want me to do—unstick the machine? Anything else?'

'Well, there are telephones, and letters, and business accounts, and disputes, and things like that.'

'I see.' She didn't really, but it certainly wouldn't pay to tell this man the real state of affairs. 'Mr Macomber—would you consider it—impertinent if I were to ask how long you personally have been in the publishing business?'

'Not at all.' But there was a look of extreme caution on his face. 'I am a Professor of English Literature, Murphy—er—Miss Murphy. And I've been in the publishing business exactly—' he stopped to consult his wristwatch '—exactly three days and four hours. Any other questions before you get down to work?'

'Yes, just one more,' she sighed. 'Somewhere around here is a little red loose-leaf book labelled Computer Access Codes. Have you seen it?'

'Little red book—oh, of course. It's in Grace's desk drawer.'

'Naturally,' she sighed. The obvious place to keep
the key to all operations, out in a secretary's desk
drawer. She stretched to get up, and another thought
struck her. 'One more thing, Mr Macomber. I can't
work later than three o' clock in the afternoon on
Tuesdays and Fridays.'

'Oh?' He looked like a puzzled man who was not
about to ask a question, so she proferred the answer.

'Little League,' she told him. 'I manage a team
in——'

'In where?'

'In the city,' she submitted. For some reason it
seemed important to her to keep the location of her
home a secret. 'Never show the opponent all your
cards,' her uncle Henry said all the time.

She stood up this time and walked slowly out of
the office, unaware as she moved that he was
following her swaying figure with more than a little
interest. In fact, 'dressed better, or not dressed at
all, she'd be a tasty package,' was exactly what he
was thinking. She cut him off both mentally and
physically by closing the door between their offices.

Back in the secretarial chair she leaned back and
laughed aloud. This looked to be the easiest scheme
she had ever schemed. 'You're as good as married,
Stacy,' she muttered as she struggled with the desk
drawers.

And of course ran into her first problem. The
desk was locked. She started up from her chair,
thinking to ask him for the keys, before common
sense struck. With what he knew about the business,
he probably would have no idea at all about keys.
She dropped back in her chair, just as the intercom
buzzer rang.

'Murphy,' he said, 'no interruptions for the next
hour.'

'Yes, sir,' she acknowledged, and barely turned in

her chair before the outer door barged open and two angry men faced her, each awkwardly carrying a painting.

'I have to see the boss,' the first man announced.

'So do I,' the other added angrily. 'This—jackass is about to ruin our latest book.'

'Good morning,' she sighed. 'I'm Murphy.'

The two of them looked at each other and then at her.

'Golden,' the first man muttered. He was a short tubby fellow, who looked as if he had high blood pressure. 'Art Department.'

'Smitkin,' the other man said. 'Public Relations.' He was rather a contrast to Golden, being medium height and thin. His nose preceded him by several inches.

'Look at this,' groaned Golden. He planted his painting across the arms of an office chair. A barely-clothed girl stood on a sandy beach in the wind, peering out to sea. The other man usurped another chair. His picture displayed a pirate on board a ship, looking at the beach. 'The book is called *Pirate's Pride*. Obviously we have to have a pirate on the cover, right? I need to see Macomber.'

Beth grinned at them both. 'Nobody sees Macomber,' she said in a soft, conspiratorial voice. 'He's practising his putting.'

'Oh God, what are we going to do?' Golden groaned. 'We have to have a decision by one o' clock, and nothing's moving in the entire building!'

'I know you're both experts in your field,' she sighed, 'but from the standpoint of an ordinary reader, I don't see why you just don't combine the two. Put them both in, why not?'

'Why not?' groaned Smitkin. 'Harry?'

'Why not?' the other man sighed. They picked up their paintings and started for the door.

'Just a minute,' Beth called. She had found a letter-opener in the only unlocked drawer of the desk. 'I need a little muscle.'

Surprisingly, it was Golden who came around the desk, banged the point of the letter-opener in under the lock, and wrenched the whole thing open as if he had done it many times before. 'My desk sticks,' he said sombrely, 'I practise regularly. Murphy? You're a great deal better at this than your predecessor.'

'You mean Grace? I thought she'd been here a long time?'

'About two months. See you later.' The two of them went out of the door, arguing gently with each other. A step or two down the corridor Smitkin came back. 'He doesn't play golf,' he informed her, 'but any gag that works is a good one. Have a good day.'

Beth closed the door behind them, and went back to her desk. No doubt about it, she told herself, this is going to be one wild job. Why won't the man see his staff? What's he doing in there that's so secret?

She started to look through the drawers, but the telephone kept ringing. Exasperated, she put all four incoming lines on hold, and went about her business. The book she wanted was in the back of the second drawer down. *Halmen Software Supergram,* the cover said. She flipped the pages until she came to the section marked 'Codes and Passwords'.

There was one code-word that unlocked all the terminals, giving them access to the central computer. 'Work', the word was. She wheeled her chair around, checked her own terminal, and typed 'Menu'. Her screen immediately lit up and returned a query. 'Lock/Unlock', it said. She typed in the code-word 'Work', and all over the building she could hear terminals buzzing into action. On her own screen the computer was displaying the list of different accounts available. The last one numbered one hundred and sixty-two.

'Good Lord,' she mumbled. Each one with its own code-word, too. This crazy business is so compartmentalised that the right hand doesn't even know what the right hand is doing, never mind the left! It made an interesting discovery, but there were other things to be done, including a very full 'In' basket, four ringing telephones, and a suspicious silence from next door.

Although she hated to do so, Beth gave the telephones priority. The first two calls were simply handled. Suppliers wanted information. She queried the computer and referred them to the proper department. The third caller was more difficult to deal with.

'Hello?' A child's voice. A fairly young child.

'This is Miss Murphy, can I help you?'

'I don't think so. I need to talk to Uncle Richard.'

'Uncle Richard? You may have the wrong number. Who is this?'

'This is Althea Macomber, that's who. I need to talk to Uncle Richard.'

Beth nibbled on her lip. She needed desperately to make a good impression on Mr Macomber during these first few days. There was little enough time to do what she had to do. And to let a call get through against his specific orders? But then, it's a member of the family.

Every good secretary walks a narrow line. She must deal for her boss, and with her boss, and sometimes the two goals are not compatible. She flipped a mental coin, and pushed his buzzer. He answered, but angrily.

'I said no calls or interruptions,' he grumbled. Beth stuck her tongue out at him.

'Miss Althea Macomber is on line two,' she said quickly.

'Oh—Althea—of course.' She watched the proper light go out, indicating he had picked up his telephone, and then she disconnected her own and dived into the 'In' basket.

Half of the material was mail, some of it dated thirty days past. Beth opened the envelopes, threw away the advertisements, and arranged the remainder in some sort of sequence. Under the pile of mail she found a stenographer's notebook, with two untyped letters in it. She was bashing away at her wordprocessor when Richard Macomber came out into her office and stopped.

She stopped as well, and looked up at him with questioning eyes. 'Lunch,' he said.

'Yes.'

'I mean, lunch,' he repeated. 'As in you and I.'

'I was *working,*' she said very formally.

'I know that, but you do eat, don't you?'

'Yes,' she admitted, 'but hardly ever with the boss.'

'So you'll make an exception today,' he announced. 'This is a business lunch.'

'Oh.'

'Don't overwhelm me with your enthusiasm,' he snorted. 'I have discovered that executive secretaries are worth their weight in gold—and you look as if you could put on a little weight. I've been listening to you referee the arguments out here, and now I think it's time you paid attention to the head man.'

'There's a great deal here that needs your attention,' she argued. He waved it all away.

'There's a little girl waiting for us at India Wharf. That's more important. Come on.'

'I'm not really sure this falls under the heading of business,' she said stubbornly. 'I don't think I want

to get involved with some little girl on a wharf.
What in the world is she doing there? She ought to
be in school!'

'Ought to be,' he muttered disconsolately. 'If I
could discriminate between "ought to be", and "is"
I'd be a lot happier. Come on.'

It hardly seemed worth an argument. Beth tidied
up her desk, turned off her computer terminal, and
slipped back into her blazer. The very act seemed to
surprise him. His eyes widened as she moved. And
there's a distinctly hungry look in his eyes, she
warned herself. Remember what happened to Stacy!

Blushing, she followed him down the corridor to
the elevator. He looked into each office as he walked,
smiling more broadly every minute. When the
elevator door opened he was definitely Cheshire-cat-
style. 'Does my heart good to see all that work going
on,' he explained as he pushed the proper buttons.
'I thought when I came that my father had gone
mad—with all this electronic garbage.'

'Ms Berman didn't think so,' said Beth, without
thinking.

'Oh, my God, the Editor-in-Chief? She came up?'

'Yes. She had a small problem. I told her to do
whatever she thought was best. Isn't that all right?'

'All right? Perfect! She scares me, that one.'

Yes? I'll bet she doesn't, Beth told herself. Look
at you. You wouldn't be scared if King Kong came
in with an original manuscript.

'You are definitely a pearl without price,' he
muttered. The elevator came to a stop on the ground
floor and the door opened slowly in a stuttering
motion, to reveal to the waiting crowd the sight of
the boss kissing his secretary with considerable
enthusiasm.

Beth was still spluttering as he took her elbow
and hurried her through the lobby. And he, monster

that he was, was laughing. 'I don't think that's the least bit funny!' she snarled at him. There was a grey limousine waiting for them at the kerb.

'Not the least bit,' he assured her as he squeezed in beside her. Squeezed, she noted vaguely. The seat is wide enough for four—why are we squeezed together like this? What a stupid thing that was, to let him kiss her—publicly, at that!

'I don't appreciate that kissing business,' she snapped as the chauffeur headed up towards State Street, and the underpass beneath the Fitzgerald Freeway.

'No, of course you don't,' he said solicitously. 'I don't either. My nose still hurts. It wouldn't have happened if you had been a proper elderly lady. But no, you had to turn out to be a beautiful spitfire. Murphy, sometimes we men get blamed for things that are just not naturally our fault.'

'I don't understand you, and I don't want you to explain.'

'Afraid of the truth, that's what's wrong with modern women,' he sighed dolefully. 'But I'm going to explain, anyway. If Nature hadn't designed you in such a delightful package—purely in the interest of propagating the race, you understand—we men wouldn't always be faced with temptation. Now, look what you do to that perfectly innocent blouse!'

'I said I didn't want to hear,' she returned frantically. 'It's not something I *do,* it's just something I *am.* And I don't care to continue this subject.'

'I see that,' he chuckled. 'Here we are.' The limousine came to a stop, and he helped her out. They were standing just in front of two massive apartment towers, each far enough apart from the other so that both had a magnificent view of the harbour.

'You lunch here?' she asked, astonishment overcoming her.

'I lunch here,' he announced. 'And breakfast here. And sometimes, God willing, I sleep here.'

She skidded to a halt, despite the pressure of his hand on her elbow. 'Oh no, Mr Macomber. You don't get me alone in your apartment, not for anything.'

'Whatever are you thinking about, Murphy?' She glared up at him. There was a crinkle of a smile around the corners of his mouth. 'We certainly won't be alone. My niece is waiting for us upstairs. Come along, there's a nice girl.'

His hand urged her along. She went quietly, *like a nice girl!* He needs someone to prick that terrible windbag of ego, she told herself as he hurried her along. Very suddenly, although her resolve remained, her ability to slay Stacy's dragon was becoming more and more questionable in her own mind.

The lobby at Harbor Towers was quiet, presided over by a reception desk. Almost out of sight in one of the corners, she could see a uniformed guard. The elevator whisked them upwards in seconds—just how high Beth could not see. There were no groans and rattles, just instant acceleration that left her stomach two floors behind them. She was gasping when the door opened, and ejected them into a quiet corridor with two doors showing. He guided her in through the left-hand door.

'Good God!' she muttered.

'Indeed,' he agreed. They were standing in the middle of a sunken living-room. Two of the walls were entirely windows, filled with the grey and sunlight of the busy harbour. I could put my whole house in here and still have room for a hot-dog stand, she thought.

'Bathroom to your right,' he told her. 'I'm sure

you want to do whatever it is women do.'

'I'm sure I do,' she snapped back at him. 'May I have my arm back?'

He seemed to have forgotten he was still clutching her. His fingers relaxed, and she moved away from him, rubbing circulation back into the fingers of her hand.

'Say, that was careless of me, and I apologise,' he said. That soft voice, sweet as syrup, was back. And so was the gleam in his eye. She had meant to say something sarcastic. After measuring his look, she gave it up and fled, slamming the bathroom door behind her. How can he *do* that to me? she thought, leaning her back against the door. He's all bandaged up like a mummy, and he *still* is the most macho —damn. *No wonder Stacy is in trouble.* A sober thought, heavy enough to bring her feet back down on to the plush rug. Even in the bathroom, she thought. Plush rugs. Damn the man!

She spent very little time splashing cold water on her face, scrubbing her hands, examining her arm, where the marks of his fingers were still visible. She spent a very great deal of time putting her mental house back in order. So it was almost fifteen minutes later that she came out of the bathroom, and followed the voices around a corner to a massive dining-room, facing the harbour. An elderly woman was standing at what had to be the kitchen door, watching while four feet of husky little girl carefully set a tray on the huge table. Food enough for twenty, Beth told herself.

Richard Macomber came in her direction, and grabbed her arm in the same spot as before. She winced, but he hardly seemed to notice, towing her along behind him towards the middle of the room.

'Mrs Moore, this is my new secretary, Murphy. She doesn't have a first name.'

The elderly woman flashed him a warning stare. 'Emily,' she said softly. 'I'm the family housekeeper.'

'Beth,' she answered, in the same spirit. 'I'm—I don't know *what* I am at the moment.'

The little girl had finished her task, and came back around the table to stand with hands on hips, staring. Beth had the sick feeling that she was being evaluated, and failing. The freckles on the girl's nose seemed to have joined ranks, almost forming lines. Her shoulder-length blonde hair was almost platinum, and her teeth were too big for her mouth. 'My God,' the child said, 'is that the best you can do, Uncle Rich?'

CHAPTER THREE

'YOU'LL not forget I have to leave?' his housekeeper reminded him. 'My sister is that ill.'

'She isn't even pretty, Uncle Rich.'

'That's *enough,* Althea. What time will you be back, Mrs Moore?'

'And she don't wear pretty clothes.'

'I won't be back today, I don't think. And tomorrow is my day off.'

'Althea, if you say one more word I'll tan your bottom! That will be all right, Mrs Moore. We'll take care of the dishes and things.'

'You don't have to come on the heavy uncle on my account,' said Beth as the housekeeper walked out of the room. 'I'm sure the little girl is perfectly right.'

'The little monster is *not* right,' Richard Macomber announced to the world in a very loud voice. 'Sit down, brat!'

'He means me,' muttered Althea, as Beth made a move towards a chair. 'I wish my daddy was here.' Real tears touched the corners of the child's eyes.

'Well, so do I. For once we agree on something.' Her uncle glared at her, and came around to hold Beth's chair. 'I don't know why I agreed to all this crazy business in the first place. You and your brother are a prize pair!'

'You won't get anywhere talking like that,' Beth said softly. 'Child-raising can't be done with just a loud mouth,' she told him very firmly.

'So you think you can bring things right with a soft answer?'

'I don't think—it's none of my business,' she sighed. 'I'm a secretary, not a nanny. And believe me, there are enough problems in my own family without me taking on your family.'

'Althea, eat your soup.' The lunch was quickly demolished. Thick tomato soup, followed by bacon-lettuce-tomato sandwiches, BLTs as they are known in New England. The little girl had a healthy appetite, and Beth was feeling hunger pains, too. When it was all over, the uncle pushed his plate away, and tapped Althea on the shoulder.

'Now, young lady, we'll hear why it is you're home from school in the middle of the day?'

'I don't like that school,' the girl muttered, ducking her head. He lifted up her chin with one big finger.

'Why are you home in the middle of the day?'

'They're having ballet classes this afternoon, that's why. They want me to—I ain't going to put on one of those stupid little dress things. I just can't do that.'

'Well, that's all really beside the point,' he said gruffly. 'You'll have to go back this afternoon.'

'I—can't do that.'

'And why not?' He was back up to a roar by this time. Beth winced, and covered her ears.

'After I kicked Sister Mary, the Principal said something like "suspension for the rest of the week", and you have to come and see her Thursday afternoon, or else——'

'Or else what?'

'I—don't remember what. But I won't like it.'

He shook his head in disgust. 'I thought I had enough trouble raising your father——Well, Mrs Moore won't be here this afternoon, and I certainly can't leave you here alone.' They both looked expectantly at Beth.

'I wish you would both stop shouting at each other,' she said grimly. 'I have sensitive ears. Am I supposed to come up with a solution?'

'That's why you have the title, Executive Secretary,' he returned.

'There's that little alcove in my office, with a television set,' she suggested. 'Perhaps Miss Macomber could——'

'That's it,' he snapped. 'Under the eagle eye of Murphy!'

'I don't think that's a good idea,' grumbled Althea. She was still mumbling as the limousine took them back to Liberty Square.

The two Macombers went through into his inner office for *further discussions,* he said. The little girl looked as if she were up on execution block, but Beth had enough problems of her own. The afternoon mail had come, burying her desk under its load. She set about categorising, to be interrupted twice by inter-department squabbles that took more diplomacy than knowledge. She settled them, and then decided to take a break in the Ladies, down at the end of the hall. It was already occupied—by a lovely-looking little Oriental girl of about twenty, crying her eyes out.

'My name is Murphy,' offered Beth. 'Can I help?'

'Nobody can help,' the girl sobbed.

'Probably. But if you feel like telling me about it?'

The girl looked up at her, dabbing at her eyes with a tiny handkerchief. 'He keeps chasing me around the office,' she returned. 'He just won't leave me alone.'

'Who?'

'Brent. Mr Brent, in Personnel.'

'Surely there's something than can be done?'

'No. You know what a reputation Mr Macomber has.'

'No, I'm afraid I don't.'

'He's a—a playboy. That's why people like Brent think they can get away with *anything.*'

Of course, Beth told herself. What would you expect? Ramrod Macomber, just back from Cornell. Stacy. Poor Stacy. And his little niece! What a truly terrible monster this man is! And for a while there, this morning, I almost thought he might be—human!

She walked over and patted the girl on the shoulder. 'There's always something that can be done,' she said firmly. 'What's your name? Margie? All right, Margie, you stay here for a half-hour or so, and then go back to your job. I guarantee that there will be changes.

Margie looked up at her through her tears. 'You really think so?'

'I really think so.' Full of crusading spirit, Beth went back up the hall, just in time to meet Althea being ushered out of the inner office.

'Hold all my calls for an hour, Murphy,' he said. 'And keep an eye on this little brat.' The child walked sullenly over to the alcove, turned on the television set, and lost herself among the million cartoon shows that pepper the afternoon air in Boston. *Which is just what I need,* Beth told herself. She picked up the in-house telephone and called Personnel.

Within six minutes the Personnel Director was stalking indignantly into her office. 'I'm not some copy reader, to be whistled up here at a moment's notice,' he said sharply.

'No? Close the door behind you. Sit down, Mr Brent.' She sat back in her chair, twirling a pencil in her hands, watching as he got progressively more nervous.

'Well?' he offered tentatively.

'Not well at all, Mr Brent,' she said coldly. 'I've been checking your record.' She gestured with her pencil towards the screen of her computer terminal. 'Mr Macomber is so—upset by the whole affair that he asked me to handle the problem.'

'What problem? I want to see the boss.'

'That's your privilege,' she smiled, leaning over towards the intercom box. 'Although he did say something about—"breaking his damn neck", I think the exact words were.'

'No——' The man was perspiring profusely. 'I—don't bother him.'

'I'm surprised, Mr Brent. You have a wife and two children, and you've been with the firm for eighteen years. Too bad.'

'Too bad?'

'Is it too warm in here, Mr Brent?'

'I—no.'

She settled back in her chair again. 'We have received a complaint, Mr Brent. Sexual harassment, it's called. Too bad. And I suppose we'll have to notify your wife, as well as all the rest of——'

'All the rest of——?'

'Well, I'm sure you know. It's a criminal complaint, Mr Brent. The police, newspapers, public prosecution—all that—are you ill?'

'I—surely—but—eighteen years of service! Surely Mr Macomber doesn't——?

'Mr Macomber was all for calling the police as soon as he heard. I managed to calm him down. You were saying?'

'I—it wasn't intentional—it was—I certainly don't think it would happen again!' There was such a pleading in his voice that Beth, hard heart and all, was *almost* touched.

'If we could be sure of that?'

'I—I guarantee it!'

'Well, perhaps I could talk to Margie, and see if she wants to suspend the complaint. You understand what that means? One slip—one more bit of this—and I automatically start making calls. And Margie will be in direct contact with me at all times. You *do* understand?'

She smiled again as he scuttled out of the office. A thin smile. Beth Murphy was as much a Women's Libber as anyone who carried a sign at the State House. And she had done that, too.

She was still smiling when Richard Macomber came out of his office. He was smiling, too.

'Who's running this place?' he asked jovially.

'Why, whatever do you mean?' she returned.

'You must have accidentally left the key up on your intercom set. I heard that whole thing. Brent playing games again, was he?'

'He's done it before?'

'I heard rumours. Scorched his tail, didn't you?'

'Whatever do you mean?' she repeated. 'There are a dozen letters you have to look at.'

'You mean, you haven't answered them yourself?'

'Now, how could I do that, Mr Macomber? I'm only your secretary!' And as for leaving the key up on the intercom, why should I tell him it was far from accidental? She had that thin smile back on her face again as she followed him into his office with her hands full of mail to be answered.

They were barely inside the room when Richard Macomber wheeled around and snatched her up in his arms. Her notebook and the letters scattered all over the carpet, and her mind went blank as he gently touched her lips with his. For just a second she relaxed, enjoying the contact, the taste of honey. And then she remembered who she was, and what *he* was.

She pushed away from him. His hands seemed to release her reluctantly. Her face was red with the anger of it all as her hands fumbled to bring her blouse out of its disarray.

'I don't know what you think you're doing,' she spluttered at him. 'I came here as a secretary, not as some—some——' Words failed her.

'Hey, it was only a *thank you* thing,' he said, perturbed. 'If I'd known it would bring *this* on——'

'I don't need this sort of thanks. If it happens again, you'll not only need a new secretary, but I'll see that you're blackballed in every temporary help office in the city. Is that clear, Mr Macomber?'

That's *very* clear,' he agreed. 'You said you had some letters?'

'I'll give him one thing, though,' Beth muttered as she walked into her own home at the end of the day. 'When given a good briefing, he makes decisions in a hurry. This staff needs to be whipped into shape, but there's nothing wrong with Richard Macomber—as an executive, that is. And it's easy to see how he got his reputation. He could charm the birds down out of the trees!'

'What did you say, Aunt Beth?'

'Nothing, Stacy. Did you have a good day?'

'Sort of. It was quiet around here. Did you talk to Roddy?'

'I only met him today, love. This will take a little while to arrange. Did you fix this spaghetti? How nice. And by the way, we really should have you go see a local doctor. A complete check-up. What say, Stacy?'

Her niece looked at her peculiarly. 'I just had one a month ago,' she said cautiously.

'So you can have another,' Beth laughed. 'It pays

to have a second opinion. Did you call your mother or father?'

Stacy ducked her head, hiding behind her beautiful blonde hair. 'I—tried,' she mumbled, 'but there was no answer—or something.'

Beth shrugged her shoulders. All she had ever read about such cases indicated an initial period of upset. She made no more mention of it as she devoured the slightly under-cooked meal.

It wasn't until two hours later, having conferred briefly with Mary by telephone, that Beth realised how tiring the day had been. She was in the shower, letting the hot water run over her tense shoulder muscles. When they relaxed, she almost sagged into the wall. 'And it's all Macomber's fault,' she muttered as she shampooed her hair.

It really must have been. There was certainly no *other* reason why his face bothered her dreams all that night, and far into the early morning.

Beth was up early, despite the poor night. A cup of coffee at seven-thirty, and a quick check on Stacy, who was huddled up in her bed, cuddling the old teddy bear, a family heritage. 'Lord, she's only a baby herself,' sighed Beth, as she quietly shut the door and called a taxi for herself.

Only the doorman was on duty at Liberty Square, but he had all the keys, and welcomed her. 'Sam. Sam Hrudneck,' he introduced himself. All five feet of him sparkled with cleanliness and enthusiasm. Before she managed to get by, Beth had heard all about his home in the Old Country, his children, and his sick wife. She listened closely; it was her stock in trade. Upstairs in the office she stripped off her brown blazer—the one that matched her brown skirt, and set to work. The place needed organisation in some places, and disorganisation in others. She pulled out the computer's instruction book, did a quick study of a couple of pages, and punched in a code-word that would permanently unlock the main computer bank itself. As she thumbed through the loose-leaf booklet, a plan was forming hazily in her mind.

By nine o'clock she had solved the mail problem. 'But it's always been this way,' the receptionist wailed. 'All the mail, except for manuscripts, goes directly to Mr Macomber's office.'

'So it will be a change,' Beth said crisply. 'Not too soon around here, either. I don't understand how a firm that publishes all these skin-novels could be so far behind the times in administration. From now on, you sort the mail, send it to the department heads, and let them worry about it. The only things that come to Mr Macomber are complaints and personal mail.'

The receptionist was not too sure about anything, but looking up at Beth, drew a little assurance. 'I—yes, Mrs Murphy.'

'Miss Murphy, if you please. Now, where is the Editor's office?'

'Editor? We have six of them, Miss Murphy.'

'Six editors? Good lord. I thought the editor was in charge of everything?'

'Oh, her! You mean the Editor-in-Chief. We have an editor for each of the six different kinds of books we print. Miss Berman is the Editor-in-Chief. She's on the fourth floor, room 402.'

Beth took a quick check on the time. Nine forty-five. Too late to pursue *that* particular line of enquiry. Macomber would be looking for her. And isn't that strange? she thought. I've never had any trouble before, thinking politely about the bosses I've worked for. But this man—he doesn't deserve the title Mister. Just—Macomber. She brushed the thought out of her mind and went striding over to the elevator, not at all aware of the man who followed close behind her, admiring the flash of her lovely long legs, which no amount of brown skirt could hide.

Her mind occupied by many trails of thought, she paid no attention until after the elevator door wheezed shut. It gave a lurch, and began to creep upward.

'Good morning, Murphy,' he said, so close behind her that she jumped. She whirled around, backing into a corner. The floor beneath her feet stuttered, swayed, and stopped. The door remained closed.

'My——'

'Goodness,' he supplied, with a chuckle. 'We seem to have a problem.'

'Yes,' she gasped. The bandage was gone from his cheek, leaving a tight-stitched scar, a good balance to the scratch marks on the other side. His nose was still partly covered, but with a skin-tinted Band Aid. 'Pirate,' she muttered, unconscious of what she was saying.

'How did you know?' He was glaring at her, the glint in those deep brown eyes like a danger signal. Glaring, and moving close enough to tower over her.

'How did I know what?' she managed to squeak.

'Pirate,' he snapped. 'How the hell did you know I was writing that series?'

'Writing? I don't know what you're—I—*Pirate's Pride?*'

'Yes, damn you, *Pirate's Pride!*'

'That's an awful book,' she whispered.

'Yes,' he roared, 'and it will sell a half-million copies. How did you know?'

'I—all that sex, and stuff. I—I didn't finish it.'

'So I'm worried,' he snarled. 'If one word of this leaks out, I'll be the laughing stock of Boston. What gave it away?'

'It's wasn't hard,' she told him. 'That business about being locked up in your office. Hah! What could a Professor of Literature be doing all barricaded away from people?'

'Well, nobody else ever noticed,' he snapped.

'And then, for a man who's only been working here a week or so, you knew an awful lot about the books—when you were answering the letters,' she added reflectively.

'So there's no use trying to pull wool,' he said sheepishly. The grin, that little boyish thing that pulled at one corner of his mouth, was back again. 'What will it cost to keep my secret?'

'Cost? I don't understand you.'

He sighed, as if explaining were beneath him. 'I don't want to see the story in every gossip column, and I'm willing to pay a reasonable amount of maintain my privacy.'

'Not to me,' she snapped indignantly. 'You hired a secretary. A secretary keeps her secrets. I wouldn't think of accepting money for anything like that. What's happening to the elevator?'

'It appears to be stopped between floors,' he returned. 'We can either sit here until someone comes along to fix it, or we can climb out. Your choice.'

My choice, she thought. To sit in this little box with him? She glanced around the little six-foot cube. The dark walls bore the mark of the early twenties. The ornate brass buttons sparkled, even if they didn't work. The floor was bare. In the corner was a little plaque. 'Otis Elevators', it said, '1924'. And I'm penned up in this thing with him? There ought to be a law. Even all battered and abused he's a sexy sight. Who knows what would—and then there's Stacy!

'I'd prefer to climb out, Mr Macomber.'

'My name is Richard,' he tendered. By now Beth had rearranged her thinking, was back in control. And just a little bit angry.

'I thought they called you Ramrod.'

'That was a long time ago,' he returned. 'You've been checking up on me?' She turned her head away, but both his hands landed on her shoulders and turned her back again. 'You *have* been, you little devil. Nobody's called me Ramrod since my undergraduate days at Yale. I played football back then. A long time ago. And you've dug it all up. I wonder why?'

Beth stuck out her chin at him, mustered up a steel-like stare, and refused to answer. His hand moved up and slithered through her tight-bound hair. The pins began to fall out as he did so, releasing a cloud of red-gold to frame her heart-shaped face.

'Now look what you've done,' she complained bitterly.

'Wonderful!' His hands completed their mission, and then combed through her tresses. She stood flat-footed, caught by surprise, feeling the tingling as his hands moved. A tingling that she had never felt before. Seconds elapsed before she was able to throw off the hypnosis and back away.

'Don't!' she muttered. 'Don't!'

His eyes were hooded as she stared up at them. There was a look of surprise on his face. Surprise, and something else that Beth could not read. 'A disguise!' he said softly. 'You're wearing a damn disguise. It makes a fellow wonder, why?'

She did her best to brush her hair back in order, using her fingers, at the same time that she stooped and felt along the floor for her lost hairpins. He squatted down beside her, with the natural ease of a born athlete. *Too close,* her brain screamed at her.

She stood up again, and backed away. 'We were going to climb out,' she said hesitantly.

'Climb out?' He looked around him, as if in a strange place. 'Oh—climb out. Yes.' He walked over into the far corner of the elevator, stripped off his tan sports jacket, bent his knees a couple of times as if to warm them up, and jumped. His upstretched hands pushed against a square trapdoor in the roof, and brushed it aside. Another second or two, as he caught his breath and judged, and he jumped again.

This time his hands went through the opening and caught on to its sides. His arm muscles flexed, drawing him up effortlessly into the hole in the roof, and he was gone. Beth stared at the place he had just occupied. The empty space. Tarzan, the ape-man? An Olympic-class gymnast? She was still shaking her head as he reappeared, looking down at her. 'Come on,' he offered, extending both hands down in her direction.

'Come on?'

'For God's sake, lady. Jump!'

She moved over under him, staring up uneasily. 'Jump? There's no way in the world I can jump that high,' she snarled.

'Only as far as my hands,' he chuckled. It was the laugh that did it. That, and the grin on his face. Swearing under her breath, she flexed her own body, warmed up in place, and jumped. Not high enough to reach the roof, but high enough for two steely claws to latch on to her extended wrists, and to pull her effortlessly up out of the elevator box and on to its roof. She was too frightened to pay any attention to the ripping sound as the three top buttons on her blouse were torn off.

'Nice,' he said, holding her in position in front of him.

'What in the world are you——?' She followed

his eyes—downward—to where her lacy blouse lay open, all the way to her navel. Pulled out of her skirt by the effort, laid bare by the lack of buttons, and putting her breasts on full display. The filmy half-bra that she wore did nothing to conceal. It was never meant to.

'Stop that!' she shouted at him, totally embarrassed. Her right hand swung in the direction of his scarred cheek, and landed squarely on the stitches.

'Hell fire,' he roared as he staggered back, out of the line of fire. 'I was only *looking,* not *raping,* lady!' His left hand came up to cradle his aching wound, and Beth was entirely undone.

'Oh, my!' she moaned. 'I—I didn't mean to hit your—you. I—please. I apologise. I——'

'OK,' he muttered. 'So it was an accident on both sides. Next time you swing at me, hit me in the stomach or something. Come on, we still have a way to go.'

She looked up at the elevator shaft. They were exactly half-way between floors, and must now climb up another six feet to the doors on the second floor. 'I'm not sure I can climb that far,' she gasped.

'No problem,' he returned. 'Hold on to this.' He wrapped both her hands around the greasy cable that suspended the car. It's good support, she told herself, and I'll worry about the grease later. He was looking at their climbing problem, and in just a few quick movements, was standing on the door ledge above them, pushing at the release handle. The doors gave a dismal sigh, and swung open. He dropped back down, on to the top of the elevator. 'Your turn,' he told her.

She had trouble getting her hands to unlock from the cable. It was a moment of safety she just did not want to lose. 'Come on now.' His lips were at her ear, his hands at her waist. 'Come on now. Everything's all right.' She managed to relax enough to come free from the cable, and he ushered her over to the wall. 'And up you go.' His hands on her waist lifted her just far enough for her to grab the door handles. She hung on there, not sure what to do next.

His hands slipped down from her waist to her thighs, under her skirt, and lifted again. Even in a stupid position like this, she thought, he turns me on. Those damn hands! The added height was just enough. She scrambled upward, getting her feet on to the corridor floor, and squeezed herself out of the elevator shaft. He was up and beside her before she could stand up, his warm hands under her shoulders, setting her up on her feet.

Footsteps thundered down the hall behind them as she threw her greasy hands around his neck, and offered him her own version of a thank-you kiss. It was as warm and as full and as passionate as she was herself, and he responded in kind.

'Uncle Rich, what are you doing?' The words shocked Beth back to normal. Her hand slipped off his neck, smearing him liberally with the grease as she came down off her toes, and moved away from him. Althea was standing in the forefront of the little crowd, staring at them both.

'We got stuck in the elevator,' Beth managed to gasp.

'Yeah, and that ain't all,' the little girl said solemnly. 'Why don't you leave my uncle alone!'

'I—I will,' squeaked Beth, then looked down at herself and groaned. The blouse was beyond repair. In addition to being buttonless, it was smeared with grease, and flecks of blood. Not her blood, but Richard's. His cheek was bleeding slowly.

'Oh, my God,' she muttered, fumbling for the tiny

handkerchief she always carried in the pocket of her skirt.

'Don't bother,' he said calmly. 'You're getting more grease on the damn thing.'

'Well, I can't help that.' Her emotions had been stretched too far, and the tears began to roll. 'It's all your fault, anyway.'

'Yes, of course it is,' he answered sarcastically. 'Why my fault?'

'Because it's your damn elevator!' she snarled. Her hands, previously hanging at her sides, made a futile effort to close the gaps in her torn blouse.

'Yeah,' he snarled. 'Why didn't I think of that? Sweeny! Where the hell is—Sweeny, damn you, get that elevator fixed!'

'You don't have to growl at them,' Beth managed through her tears. 'Just because—oh!' He swept her up in his arms and stalked through the crowd, Althea following behind them, skipping to keep up.

He slammed the office door closed behind them, and put Beth down on her trembling feet. Trembling with anger, not fear. 'Look, what a mess!' The words were trying to tumble out too fast for her tongue to handle.

'No doubt about it,' he sighed, out of breath. 'I'm getting out of shape. You'll have to go home, Murphy. Take the rest of the day off. My car is downstairs. Only——'

She had managed to dry her tears, tuck the remnants of her blouse back in her skirt, and wipe her hands off on paper towels. And had time to think. Forget the hands, she told herself. The warm, strong hands on her wrists, on her waist, on her thighs. Forget the crazy feeling it all inspired. Forget the look in his eyes. Forget the kiss. Remember Stacy. 'Only what?'

'Only—I have to go back to my doctor's, and I'd

prefer not to take Althea with me. Could you?'

'Take her home with me?'

'Yes. The chauffeur can stay with you, and bring her along—say about four o'clock?'

Beth's mind was ticking on all cylinders by this time. Tuesday, and a Little League game scheduled to start at four o'clock. 'How about six?' she suggested. 'I have something scheduled for today. You must remember that I told you on Tuesday and Friday I have to be free by three o'clock?'

'I'd forgotten.' Richard waved her protests aside. 'OK. Six o'clock. If she'll stay that long.'

'Why *should* I?' Althea wanted to know.

'Because I told you to!' he roared back at her. 'Why is it that I suddenly have to put up with *two* ornery females at the same time? I can remember my father saying that publishing was the most relaxing business in the world! I sure wouldn't be able to—don't stand there staring at me—either one of you!'

He disappeared into his inner office and came back out with a blazer in his hands. 'I keep a couple of spares,' he commented, slipping it over Beth's shoulders. 'And you can't run through the building on display like that.'

'I wouldn't be on display if it hadn't been for you,' she snapped back at him. 'The mail is all in order. Don't forget to lock the safe when you leave.'

'You'd better look out, Uncle Rich,' warned Althea.

'Had I?'

'That's the way Mommy used to talk to Dad when she was mad at him.'

'Ah! Well, Murphy is *only* my secretary, little bit, not my wife. You go along with her—and I'll see you at supper.'

Surprisingly, the child did just that.

CHAPTER FOUR

'Wow!' Althea said softly. They were at the baseball field, crouching together on the sidelines in front of the team bench. 'I didn't know you owned a baseball team!' There was even a touch of respect in her voice. It brought a smile to Beth's face.

'I don't *own* it,' she returned. 'My company sponsors the team, and I'm the manager. Here's the batting order. Would you take it over to that gentleman behind the plate?'

'The fat guy? Sure!' She was off in a burst of speed that caused Beth to think. And was back before Beth had an answer.

'Can any kid play?'

Beth was busy, sorting out her team to send it on to the field. The opposition had first bats, being the visitors. 'Here it is, Tuesday, and already I'm out of pitchers,' she muttered. 'Well—Frankie!' A tall, thin boy slouched over to her, pounding his fist into his glove. 'Frankie, you have to start for us. All our other pitchers are just not available.'

'Me? You know I can't pitch, Miss Beth. I wanna play shortstop.'

'Yes, well, *somebody* has to pitch, Frank. And you're nominated. Off you go.'

Ten minutes later, Beth was beginning to wish she were in Albuquerque. Frankie was right. At least, on this fine sunny day he was no pitcher. Six men on the opposing team had come to bat, Frankie had thrown the ball in their general direction, and not come even close to home-plate.

'He's not too good,' Althea commented. The pair of them were still kneeling on the sidelines. 'Can any kid play?'

Beth broke her concentration, and looked over at the girl. 'Anybody between eight and twelve, who's registered with the League,' she said. 'Think you know how to play?'

'Oh, I've had a game or two,' Althea returned. She sported a big grin on her face. Like her uncle, Beth thought. She's up to something!

'Did you want to play?'

'I wouldn't mind—but I'm not registered, right?'

'Yes, but the Player-Agent of the League is sitting right over there, and we're two players short. Yes or no?' After all, we can't hardly do any worse than we're doing, she told herself, moments later, as she walked around the back of the cage and caught up with Mr Hendricks.

'Some fireballing substitute?' Mr Hendricks was somebody's grandfather, a bent, sparse-haired gentle man, full of laughter. 'No reason why we can't register him right now. Name?'

'It's a *her*,' Beth responded, and provided the rest of the details. Her team was behind, six to nothing, by the time she walked the dusty way back to her own bench. 'You can play, Althea. I've a couple of team jerseys in the duffel bag. Go slip into one—and a hat. You have to have a hat.' The girl rushed off.

'And nobody out?' The two boys nearest her on the bench made a noise associated with the Bronx.

'At this rate it'll be dark before we even get up to bat,' one of them snapped. And by that time Althea was back, a blue and gold jersey covering her blouse, and her blonde hair tucked up under a cap.

'Now, I'm ready,' the girl said. There was a gleam of excitement in her voice. 'Put me in?'

'Where, Althea?'

'On the ball field they call me Al,' she returned. 'I'm a pitcher.'

'You?'

'Believe it. Where can I warm up?'

Beth gestured behind her. Their reserve catcher got up, settled his mitt on his hand, and led the girl behind the dug-out. In the back of her mind Beth heard and measured the satisfactory thuds as a ball, thrown with speed behind her, slapped its way into a glove.

The score was nine to nothing, with one out, when the fans in the bleacher seats began to get impatient. 'Put in Number Thirty-Six,' they started chanting. Since Beth had no Number Thirty-Six she shrugged her shoulders and watched grimly. Frankie, on the pitcher's mound, looked over at her pleadingly, and a very satisfied voice next to her ear said, 'I'm ready.'

Beth tossed her a smile, and then took a second look. With her hair put up under her cap Althea looked like a chunky boy. Her forehead was rimmed with perspiration, her jaw was working at double-speed on a stick of chewing-gum, and the number thirty-six was emblazoned across her chest. Well, what the heck, Beth told herself. How could it get worse? She stood up gracefully, to cheers from the fans, and signalled the umpire for a time-out. She walked out to the mound, took the ball from Frankie, and handed it to Althea.

'Just do the best you can,' she sighed. 'You don't need any signals. Just throw it wherever the catcher holds his glove. Right?'

'Not to worry, Miss Beth——' There was a great deal of silence as she walked back to the bench. The Rentasec team, in last place, hardly ever drew a crowd. Their opponents, The Badgers, were in first place. Althea went through her obligatory ten warm-up pitches, waved from the mound, and threw her first ball. The batter waved ineffectually, the catcher grunted as the incoming pitch knocked him off his feet, and the game went on.

By the fourth inning the score was still nine to one. Not a single additional batter from The Badgers had got on base since Althea had begun to pitch, but unfortunately it wasn't only pitching that suffered on Beth's team. The opposing pitcher was no ball of fire, but her young men were unable to hit what he offered.

'So this is what you're up to!' The voice was right in her ear. She snapped her head around. Richard Macomber, dressed in denims and a loosely buttoned shirt, was squatting at her side. 'You're behind?'

'Nine to one,' she muttered, wishing she could sink into the ground.

'You don't look like somebody's executive secretary,' he laughed. 'That kid is going to use *that* bat?' Beth looked around. Little Roger Devlin was dragging a bat almost as big as he was.

'We don't have any smaller,' Beth muttered, glaring at him. So now it's all *my* fault? she asked herself.

'Don't mutter,' he reproved. 'That's almost as impolite as whispering.' Before she could think of an answer he was up and calling the little batter over to him. There was a long discussion. The boy nodded, shifted his hands up the length of the bat, and walked over to home-plate. He swung at the first pitch offered. Swung, and knocked the ball smartly back up the middle of the field, where it zoomed by the surprised pitcher, rolled through the legs of the shortstop, and stopped half-way to the fence in centrefield.

It was the beginning of a procession. He talked to each batter before he came up to the plate, and a succession of singles put a Rentasec player on each of the bases. Althea took her turn in the batter's box. Beth didn't want to watch. It all seemed inevitable. Her team had fallen into the hands of the Macombers, and had become the Cinderella kids. She needed no roar from the fans to tell her that the little girl had just knocked the ball over the centre-field fence.

'Well now, that wasn't too bad,' Rich Macomber gloated, as the game came to a riotous end, with her team ahead fifteen to nine. The boys were jumping up and down, pounding each other on the back. Althea was the centre of attention from both her team-mates and fans, and Richard was standing close behind her as she totted up the figures in her score-book.

'Not bad at all,' she agreed, closing the book and leaning back against him. 'Considering that it's the first game we've won all year, it's a major triumph!' His arms came around her, just below the swell of her breasts, and locked her in position. It was a gentle taking.

'I think I'm getting to like my secretary more and more,' he said softly in her ear. 'In fact——' He turned her around, tilting her chin up. The sun played highlights on her two freckles, just at the base of her nose. And he kissed her.

Beth had a strange double-feeling. There was a great roar that was blocking her ears. And then there was this tender, nibbling sensation that seemed to be originating at the point of contact, where his tongue explored the inner side of her lip. It was a transferable sensation. It seemed to leap from spot to spot within her, like a little joined packet of fire-crackers, setting fires wherever it landed.

It was hard to tell when the kiss stopped and the sensations continued. She felt infinitely tired, infinitely aroused. And the roar in her ears was real.

Half the baseball fans in the park were gathered around the pair of them, cheering him on. She offered them a weak smile, and then was brought down to earth hard when her eye caught the steel glare that shone in Althea's eyes.

'What are you doing to my uncle?'

'I—I'm not doing anything to your uncle. *He's* doing it.' Beth shook her head to fight back the haziness. 'How come you don't ask *him* what he's doing?'

'C'mon, Uncle Rich. I want to go home.'

Still hugging Beth, he offered his niece one of those lopsided smiles. 'Well now,' he said, 'I didn't stand around trying to break things up when you were playing *your* game, why is it that you have to break it up when I'm playing *my* game?'

'Oh, c'mon,' Althea returned wearily. 'I'm tired. And you know what happens to you when you play that kind of game. You've been told.'

'And you were listening at the door, right?'

'Why don't you——?' Beth started, and then stopped. My God, I was about to invite them home for coffee and cookies, she snarled fiercely at herself. Just what I need, to walk in the house with *him* in tow, and Stacy moping around the place!

'Why don't you——?' he prompted, grinning.

Remember who your enemies are, she told herself, and gritted her teeth. 'Why don't you take Althea home?' she said coldly.

'Yeah, why don't you?' the girl echoed. She came over and stood just in front of Beth, with both hands on hips. 'You know, I kind of like you, Miss Beth. You'd make a fine manager, with a little more trainin', and I suppose you make a fine secretary. But Uncle Rich is the only bachelor uncle I've got left, and I don't want him spoiled with mushy stuff like that.'

'Gee, thanks a lot,' he grumbled, swinging the girl up to his shoulder, dirt and all. 'Tell you what—we'll both take Beth home, and then you and I will——'

'No, thank you,' Beth told him. Polite but cold, that's the way to treat him! 'I only live a block or two away, and I don't want you to go out of your way.' And I don't want you taking me home, learning where I live, and perhaps running into my niece. Not until I get my scheming done, Mr Macomber!

'This seems to be a losing cause,' he acknowledged. 'Sure you wouldn't want to come home with us, Beth? We could go out for dinner, spend a friendly night?'

'No—No, thank you,' she stuttered. Talk about spiders and flies and parlours—why, the man must think me a flaming fool! And having finally gathered enough fuel to really kindle her anger, she glared at them both. Richard put the little girl down on her feet, and sent her off with a pat on her bottom.

'Althea?' Beth asked. She had trouble being polite to this man, but she had to know. 'Where are her parents?'

'They've gone, Beth. Both gone.'

'Oh, my God,' she muttered. They're both gone? So why are you standing there grinning at me? The kid's an orphan, and you play it like some sort of joke! She glared at him and walked away.

Stacy was uneasy that night. She just could not remain in one place. She paced the apartment, picking up odd bric-à-brac and setting it down, and making faces at herself.

'What's the problem?' asked Beth. 'You're not feeling well?'

The girl turned on her. 'Why is it you can't get through a single sentence without asking me how I feel?' she demanded. 'I feel fine. There's nothing wrong with me.'

'I know,' Beth returned soothingly. 'It's a normal thing. But still, there are changes. You're bound to feel different.'

'I don't know what you're talking about,' her niece snarled. 'I wish I were in California!' She slammed off to her room, banging the door behind her.

'I wish you were in California, too,' Beth sighed, but there was a family burden to be borne, and that's what maiden aunts were expected to do. Time limits all actions. She had about a week and a half to bring this thing to a conclusion, and get on with her life. She huddled herself into her nightgown and robe, and sat down in the bay window to give this whole affair some serious thought.

She was no further along at nine o'clock the next morning when she arrived by taxi in Liberty Square and went into the reception. 'The elevator's been repaired,' Sam assured her as she breezed by him.

'Yeah, I'll bet,' she returned, and headed for the stairs. Half-way between the second and third floors she passed little Margie Gow, her Oriental features brightly lit. Neither stopped, but Margie mouthed a 'thank you' and hurried on. Beth marked it down in her score-book of achievements. As she passed the third floor a sudden thought brought her momentarily to a halt. *The computer system!* Foolishly or not, they all depended upon the computer. Now if I could only confirm that, find out *why,* the weapon is at hand to humble the mighty Macomber. Beth took a deep breath, and headed for the next floor up. She knew exactly how to find out.

As usual, there was nobody in the office. She did the usual morning things. Activate the computer terminal, check the 'In' basket, start the coffee perco-

lator, water the two little flowerpots of African
violets the previous secretary had left, peer into his
office to see that all was well. All was not quite as
well as expected.

There was a small sofa, part of the usual office
set-up, pushed up in a corner under the windows.
Cramped into the tiny space was Richard Macomber,
fast asleep. She tiptoed over towards him. He was
still decked out in dinner-jacket, black tie, black-
striped trousers, and a silly grin. His shoes were on
the floor. One sock had disappeared. Beth smothered
the desire to laugh; playboy, out late, she judged.
There were no blankets in sight, but a beautiful
Mexican *serape* was in use as a cover for the coffee
table. She whipped it off, covered him gently, tiptoed
out, and closed the office door behind her.

Strange, she told herself, back in her outer office.
I'm going out of my way to get revenge on this guy,
and in the meantime I worry about him sleeping
cold. I wonder where he was last night? It must have
been a wild party!

There was not a great deal of time to muse.
Instantly, at nine-thirty, as if someone had turned a
switch, her phones lit up, her terminal buzzed, and
she spent the next hour fending off people who just
had to see the boss, or offered spurious directions to
those who needed decisions. By eleven, things had
slowed. She peeped in. He was still out for the
count. Time to find out, she told herself. She
connected her telephones into the automatic
answering system and sauntered down the hall to
Room 402.

Ms Maggie Berman was a surprise. The sign on
her door said Editor-in-Chief. Beth was looking for
some elderly soul, whose grey hair reflected all the
years of experience she had accumulated. And instead
found a very sharp individual indeed, a tall thin

woman, brown-haired, brown eyes, who looked at one over the tops of a pair of half-shell reading-glasses. She was dressed in the height of fashion. Beth took a deep breath. It was time to go into her act again.

'I'm Murphy. You remember?'

'Yes. Murphy, huh? Still with us?'

'Apparently.'

'Take a chair.' The original solemn expression had fled, replaced by a homely grin. 'Meeting of the Board?'

'I—guess I don't know what you mean.'

'Come on now, Murphy. I've got ears all over this building. Right at the moment I'm still running all the books—and my grapevine tells me you're running everything else.'

'Why not?' murmured Beth. 'All's right with the world, God is in Her heaven.'

'Well said. Are we in a conspiracy?'

'No, not exactly. I'm looking for information.'

'Ask away.'

'I thought publishing houses were all manuscripts and red pencils and bright lights. This place is hag-ridden by computers. What gives?'

The editor chuckled. She had a deep, attractive voice, to match her personality. 'The wave of reform,' she said. 'Mr Macomber Senior. The old man. He got himself into the hands of the computer wizards, and couldn't escape. They convinced him it would be easier, more accurate, and cheaper, if we put all our works on the computer. To tell the truth, now that we're accustomed to it, it's all true. Our regular authors submit their works on disks—we copy them into the system, do all the editing and checking directly off the original disk. When a story is passed, it's transmitted to the printer electronically, and goes directly into type. There's a saving in time and money. A story only has to be punched out once. You can't imagine the horror stories that originate when a manuscript is typed two or three times. In fact, our authors like the idea so much—those who use word processors—that they call us on the telephone, connect their little computers to ours, and submit the books directly through the line.'

'And the savings?'

'Two places. It saves us countless numbers of filing cabinets, and then saves us a whacking amount when it's time to print. There's no need to re-punch the material for printing, you see. It comes right off the edited disk.'

Beth stopped for a minute to think that over. It *sounded* possible, and the lady in front of her was no fool. So, step two. 'But don't you defeat the purpose by having so many locked programs? One hundred and sixty-two, according to my count. How does anyone get into the accounts to work on them?'

'They get an authorisation, and get the code-word,' the editor chuckled.

'They do? How?'

'You give them out, Murphy.'

'Good lord!'

'Exactly.'

'But—why? Why all the secrecy? You're not printing revolutionary manifestos, or funny money, or something?'

'No. But remember, our computer is linked to a telephone line. Any number of crazies out there go around trying to break into company computers. And we publish one range of books—biographies of important people—that a large part of the population would like to read prior to release. Newspapers spend a great deal of time trying to bribe a phrase or two out of our junior editors. You see?'

'I'm beginning to,' laughed Beth. She was, indeed.

One hundred and sixty-two accounts, each controlled by a code-word in *her* possession. The plot was coming clearer in her own mind. But if the originators of the code-words were handy—the name of the software company—and with a little vigilance, it shouldn't take long. She thanked the editor, and wandered out into the hall. One part of her mind was conspiring; the other part was working as a normal executive secretary's would. He's going to wake up soon, with a headache bigger than the Prudential building. The hall directory listed a cafeteria on the ground floor. Ignoring the creaky elevator, she ran down the stairs, singing.

The cafeteria advertised itself from out in the hall. A mixed odour of cabbage and something floated around like a ghost, haunting the place. The little dining-room was crowded with tables, long mess-hall tables from some abandoned military post, they seemed to be. Beth drew her fingers down the top of one of them, and they came away greasy. She shuddered. There was hardly a soul in the place. Lunch was already being set out on steam tables, so that what flavour it might have had would waste away.

'You want somethin'?' the man behind the counter asked.

'Yes,' Beth shuddered. 'I want a glass of tomato juice with four shakes of bitters in it, a squeeze of lemon, salt, pepper, paprika—I guess that's all.'

'Hey, lady, this ain't a fast-food café. I don't have time to make no specialties.'

'I can see it isn't,' she said grimly. 'I happen to be Mr Macomber's secretary. Mr Macomber is waiting for this little—drink. Mr Macomber is a very impatient person.' She drew herself up to full height and glared across the counter. The man took a quick look, bit back the statement he was about to make, and set to work.

When he slapped the brimming glass out on the glass counter he looked mutinous. 'And what else? You said two things?'

'Secondly, I want to talk to the manager of this place.'

'That's me.'

'And you are an employee of Macomber Publishing?'

'What did you think I was, some guy come in off the streets?'

'You have a name?'

'Page. Frank Page. Why do you want to know?'

'So I can have it correct, Mr Page, when I address your letter of dismissal. Mr Macomber takes a dim view of people selling ptomaine poison to his staff.'

'Hey now, wait a minute——'

'No, Mr Page. I don't have time. Neither do you. I'll be back tomorrow. If this place doesn't shine with polish, with the food being cooked and displayed on time—I'll bring your dismissal letter with me, to save us both time. You dig, man?'

Page stared at her, unbelieving, as she turned and sauntered slowly out, holding the glass of juice in her hand.

It had to be the elevator this time. Nobody in her right mind tries three flights of stairs balancing a brim-full glass of tomato juice. Today the old machine was on its best behaviour. The door closed with a snap, there was only a moment of hesitation, and they proceeded upward together in gentle harmony. When the door opened at the fourth floor Beth took her first breath since entering the thing, and went down the hall to her own office.

There were four telephone messages on the answering machine. She handled them, offering the decisions under 'Mr Macomber would prefer if you would——' and the advice in her own name. By the time she had finished there were sounds of movement from within. She stood up, brushed down her beige skirt, straightened her dimity blouse, picked up the glass, and went in.

He was sitting with both feet on the floor, and his head in his hands. He barely managed to look up as she came up to him. 'Take these,' she admonished, passing him two aspirin tablets. 'And drink this.'

He did exactly as ordered. 'My God, what *was* that—that atrocity you gave me to drink?'

'It's good for you.'

'Yeah. So is castor oil, but nobody drinks the stuff these days.'

Beth slapped the palm of her hand on her forehead. 'That's what I forgot,' she giggled. 'Castor oil. I don't suppose they stock it downstairs, anyway.'

'You're trying to kill me, Murphy!'

'Not exactly,' she sighed. 'You're being done good to. In a minute or two you'll feel better. That was my grandfather's recipe.'

'How old was he when it killed him?'

'It didn't,' she said primly. 'Grandfather Murphy died of alcohol. My grandmother kept telling him that the whiskey would kill him, and it did. Cirrhosis of the liver. He died on his ninety-fifth birthday.'

'Good lord,' Macomber muttered mournfully. 'Think how long he might have lived if he didn't drink.'

'Yes, well, that's neither here nor there,' she said firmly. 'It's noontime, you have a one o'clock appointment, and you'd better toddle along to your private bathroom. You need to wash——' she crinkled her nose as if the smell bothered her '—and you need to shave, and you need a change of clothes. Shall I send someone to your home?'

'No,' he groaned. 'I've got a suit on standby. Are you perhaps Simon Legree's daughter?'

'I don't know the gentleman. My family was all from Roscanon. Was he from those parts?'

'I doubt it.' He struggled to his feet, using her shoulder as a crutch for the first few steps, and managed to make it to his bathroom. Beth straightened out the couch, returned the *serape* to its original use, and went back to her own desk.

It was too late to order lunch for him. The inexorable clock had caught up to them. Maggie Berman arrived on the scene, escorting a fluttery elderly woman—wearing a hat, of all things.

'Miss Murphy, Elda. Mr Macomber's executive secretary. And this is our newest best-seller author, Mrs Elda Pern.'

'How good to meet you, Mrs Pern. Mr Macomber will be ready in just a moment. He had a small problem—with the Governor, I believe.' And God forgive me for all the little lies I've told in my career, she thought. I wonder what this dear old soul writes?

'You've read my book, of course, Miss Murphy?'

'I have it at home,' she lied with a straight face, 'but haven't had a chance to finish it yet. A fantastic story.' The intercom buzzer rang, saving her soul from another lie piled on all the rest. 'Mr Macomber is ready. Won't you go in?'

Beth looked over their heads as the two women walked into the office. Half an hour had worked wonders. In a freshly pressed suit and tie, he was the very model of a gracious business host. Even the scars on his face were subdued, as if he had—oh, God—pancake make-up? She shook her head wryly. There was no end to what could go on in a publishing house. Including snooping at the door, which I intend to do until I find out——

The introductions were in hand. Richard

Macomber was up out of his chair and around the
desk, with a big smile on his face, and one hand
extended. 'Elda—Elda Pern. Welcome. I can't tell
you how much I enjoyed your last book, *Lust on a
Little Island*. It will be on the best-seller list for
months!' Oh me, Beth sighed as she closed the door.
Lust on a Little Island? That sweet lovable thing?
She must be sixty-five if she's a day!

Whatever they talked about, they were at it for
forty-five minutes, after which the three of them
came to the door, still talking. 'And Miss Berman,
our Editor-in-Chief, will take you out for a nice
lunch,' Richard Macomber was saying, 'and show
you the cover design for your new work.' He held
the smile until the two of them disappeared from
sight, then washed it off, and plumped down in the
chair by her desk.

'Oh God,' he groaned, running his hands through
his hair.

'Alcohol often brings on remorse,' Beth said
primly, sitting up tall in her chair, with her hands
folded on the desk.

'What?'

'I said—oh, nothing. What can I do for you, Mr
Macomber?'

'Well, you could help me back to the bathroom,'
he sighed. 'My feet seem to be a little unsteady.' She
came around her desk and offered him a shoulder
to lean on. It was all he needed, just a little steadying. Back in the tiny gold-walled room adjacent to
his office—too small really to call a bathroom, too
elegant to call a washroom—he went directly to the
basin, drew hot water, and washed the heavy make-
up off his face. Beth watched, fascinated. When a
girl grows up as the only female in a family of
brothers, she often acquires curious habits. This was
one of Beth's.

He came out from under the towel looking consid-
erably   more   scarred,   more   ordinary,   more
—attractive? The word tugged at Beth's mind.

'Well,' he gruffed, 'have you never seen anything
like this? You don't wear any at all, do you?'

'Oh, I manage a little lipstick on occasion,' she
chuckled. 'But it's not from vanity. I'm allergic to
practically everything on the market.'

'Now who would have thought that?' His grin
was back, along with his animal magnetism. 'You
don't need it, Murphy. And no, I wasn't out all
night boozing!'

'I—I didn't say that.'

'I know you didn't, but you were thinking it,
weren't you? I can read your face like an open book,
girl.'

'That's a cliché,' she snapped, doing her best to
dodge his inspection. 'And don't tell me you weren't
boozing, I know the symptoms too well.'

'A chequered past, huh?'

'No. I told you. An Irish grandfather, and his
million friends.'

'Come on,' he sighed, seizing on her hand and
towing her out into his office. 'I don't know why I
care about what you think, but I do. You're
mistaken, and I want you not to be. Sit.'

He almost pushed her on to the sofa. She scuttled
along it as far as she could when he joined her. One
of his arms rested on the back of the sofa, just close
enough for his fingers to play with the loose tendrils
of her hair. 'Beautiful,' he murmured, his eyes
following his fingers.

'Please,' she snapped. 'I don't——'

'I know,' he sighed, withdrawing his hand. 'You're
not that sort of girl. Whatever that sort is. By the
way, that baseball team of yours showed a lot of
spirit.'

She grabbed at the change of subject with both hands. 'They're a fine bunch of kids,' she rattled. 'If only I were a better coach, we might do——'

'Hey, I'm helping,' he interrupted. 'Have your pitchers and catchers meet me at the same place tonight at six. Can you do that?'

'I—yes, I suppose. Why?'

'Because I was a pitcher in my college years, and played a year in AAA ball.'

'But why? I don't understand.'

'Of course you don't,' he said solemnly. 'How about, Althea will really raise hell at home if I don't?'

'Oh.' And why am I disappointed? Surely I couldn't expect him to do it for me? Yes, you could, her small voice inside her head answered. You surely could!

'Comfortable now?'

'Yes, I guess.' His words had stiffened her back, put her on edge again, and he could see it. He frowned down at her.

'Now, about last night.'

'What about it?'

'Have you ever heard of the Samaritans?'

'The anti-suicide group? Yes, I've heard of them.'

'Well, last night I had a late dinner with some politicians, and then went over to the Samaritans to stand my watch. A girl called—a desperate girl. I talked to her on the telephone for five hours. I really thought I had her calmed down, but I was wrong. She told me I was a wonderful guy, and put the phone down, and tried to jump out of a fourteenth-storey window.'

'Oh my!' she gasped.

'Oh my, yes. So I went out after that and had six straight belts of Jim Beam, and came here to sleep it off.'

'I——' Beth began.

'Yes?'

'I'm sorry, Mr Macomber.'

'Richard—not Mr Macomber.'

'I'm sorry, Richard. I—completely misjudged the affair.'

He smiled at her, and stirred himself closer. 'Do that often, do you?' he asked.

'From time to time,' she admitted. 'I'm the impetuous one in our family. I'm really sorry.'

'How sorry?'

'*Very* sorry.'

'Show me.' He sat very still. Beth moved slowly, mesmerised, sliding down the slippery surface of the sofa until they were nose to nose. And she kissed him.

CHAPTER FIVE

RICHARD MACOMBER stopped by her desk at three-thirty, having invested a whole hour and a half on business. 'They named that crowd right,' he mourned. 'A board meeting. I've never been so bored in all my life.'

'One of the penalties of wealth,' Beth said, trying to hide the laughter. 'What was accomplished?'

'Every department presented a budget proposal,' he sighed.

'And then?'

'And then we adjourned to consider them. Next month we'll meet again for a decision. What are you doing?'

Her desk was overcrowded with computer run-offs, lines of figures that tailed off the top of the desk and fell to the floor. 'Just looking,' she said, pushing the mass of figures aside. 'The major advantage of computers is that you can instantly compare and analyse.'

'Huh!' he snorted. 'If the thing is that good, why don't we take a week off and let *it* run the business? Maybe even write the books?'

'I'm not qualified in book writing,' she said demurely, and turned away from him.

'Hey, none of that.' His hand swivelled her chair back in his direction. 'Come on now, get your hat and whatever, and let's get going.'

'Get going?'

'You have a terrible memory.' He shook his head in mock disgust. 'Did you tell all the pitchers on

76

your team to meet me at the park?'

'Oh yes, I did that this morning. Well, told their mothers, of course.'

'So let's get gone.'

'Me?' she squeaked, and stopped to steady her nerves. 'I—can't go. Not today. I thought you knew that.'

'No, I didn't know that. Get your hat.'

'I haven't worn a hat since I was six years old—except for my rain hat that is.'

'Well, get whatever it is you get.'

'I can't possibly go, Mr Macomber. I have a—a date.'

'So, break it.' He leaned over to toy with her hair. She jerked away from his questing fingers. 'What's so important about this so-called date?'

I'll tell you, she wanted to scream at him, but didn't. Friday is the last day of the month, and all the women will want their cheques, and somebody has to tell the computer what to do, and that someone is me!

'I can't break the date,' she said coolly. 'It's very important to me.'

'Why?' If he leans any closer I'll bite him, she told herself, and then her tongue slipped.

'It's important to me,' she repeated. 'The day after tomorrow it becomes June, and——'

'Stop right there. I don't want to hear.' There was a pained expression on his face, as if someone had suddenly pricked his balloon. He turned around and took two quick paces away from her, and two back. 'So—your date is with this Mac fellow?'

'Lord, you remembered that?'

'I remember everything,' he snapped. 'It's serious, this business between you and Mac? Of course it is.' He left no time for her to answer, but kept doggedly on, as if talking more to himself than to her. 'Mac is very important to you, and June is the month of weddings, isn't it?' There was that look again, settling in on his face. He shrugged his shoulders. 'Well, win a few, lose a few,' he sighed. He stood up straight, devoured her with his eyes, and walked out of the office. Her eyes tracked him to the door, and held there for some time after he had disappeared.

Beth went back to her figures. Comparisons. Which book did better financially than others. Which types of books did better than other types. Which authors brought in more than others. Trends. Questions. They were all there, sitting in the computer, waiting to be asked. She asked, and the machine told her more about Macomber Publishers in thirty minutes than she might have found out for herself in six years. She used the last half-hour of the day with her word processor, typing up a summary of what she had learned, and then went home.

Stacy and Mary were both waiting for her when she arrived. For some reason her niece looked better, more healthy than ever before. Mary, on the other hand, was having a nervous fit. 'I thought you would have forgotten the payrolls,' the girl in the wheel-chair said.

'Not me,' Beth laughed. 'That's why I'm home early. Tonight's the night I spend with Mac.'

'Did you want me to stay, Beth?'

'No, lord no. I'm sure you've had a busy day?'

'Like gang-busters. We're booked solidly for the next six weeks, and have four typing jobs to be done in the office. Stacy has been helping.'

'We'll put you on the payroll, love.' Beth walked over and kissed her niece, leaving her arm around the girl's shoulder. 'You go ahead home, Mary. Stacy and I will have supper and relax, and then I'll get at the payrolls.'

The two Murphys walked upstairs, arm in arm.

The girl's skin was warm to the touch. 'You've done more than typing, haven't you?'

'I went to Revere Beach,' Stacy answered. 'I sunbathed, and walked around, and——'

'And even went swimming?'

'You're crazy, Aunt Beth. After living all my life in California, you expect me to go swimming in the ocean in May—in New England?'

'Well, some brave souls do,' Beth told her. 'What shall we have for supper?'

They compromised on a pre-cooked turkey roll, heated in the microwave oven, along with frozen mixed vegetables, and a little wild rice. It was a good meal and, by dint of much control, Beth made certain *not* to ask her niece how she was feeling.

'I'll do the dishes,' Stacy offered.

'Both of them?'

'My father never acts like you do,' Stacy surprised her by stating. 'He's always so——'

'Your father is a stick-in-the-mud,' Beth returned. 'He always was, and always will be. But a genius, for all that. See, he got all the brains.'

'And you've got all the charm.'

'Well, thank you, miss.' Beth offered a very unpractised curtsey, then looked at the clock and ran for the door. MAC was sitting in his corner, ruminating over some figures. She pulled off the cover of one of the terminals and began the payroll programming. All of which brought her wearily upstairs at midnight with finger cramps. Although MAC could compute and reason and print cheques, only Beth Murphy could sign them.

She showered quietly. Stacy was already asleep. The girl was looking better these days, but needed her sleep. 'Me, too,' she chuckled to herself, but there was one more task for the day. At one o'clock in the morning, making provision for the three-hour

time difference between Boston and California, she
direct-dialled her brother Fred.

'My, you're up late,' he said. 'We were just about to
look at the tube. How's my daughter?'

'She's looking better, Fred. She went out and got
some sunshine at the beach, and she's helping with
some local typing.'

'Got the problem all analysed, I suppose?'

'I—well—yes, Fred. But I don't think you're going
to like the answer.'

'So try me.'

'What would you say if your daughter got
married?'

'Oho! That's the way the cookie crumbles. Who's
the guy?'

'I don't think you would know him, Fred. I'd
rather not deal in names. Things are very ticklish up
here at the moment. He's a—good-looking man,
with a great deal of money, and plenty of creative
talent.'

'And you approve of him—for her?'

'I don't think any of us can change her mind,
Fred. She wants to marry him.'

'Well, I hate to put a spoke in your wheel, Beth,
but the girl's only eighteen. Weddings are out.'

'I think we might not have much to say about it,
Fred.'

'Then I'll have to depend on her aunt to look
after her for us, won't we!'

'You know I'll do my best, Fred. But—hey, don't
hang up! That isn't all I want to talk about.'

'So it's your nickel, keep talking.'

'Fred, there's a software company called Halmen.
Do you know it?'

'Do I know it? It's on all the local news, Beth.
Actually, they have a plant just down the street from
my office. I can see the goings-on every day. The

whole damn work-force is out on strike. They've been picketing the place, sabotaging the output —you wouldn't believe what a time they're having!'

'How nice,' Beth sighed happily. The last block of stone had just fallen in place around her plan.

'How nice?'

'You wouldn't understand, brother dear. Hey, did you hear that my baseball team won a game? Actually *won* a game!'

'I think we must have a poor connection, Sis,' he laughed. 'Or you've been sampling that home-made wine again. Goodnight.'

'Goodnight,' she whispered into the mouthpiece, and then held the telephone in hand as she dreamed. Held it until the raucous sound of the beeper from the central office came on.

'I should have talked to Bessie,' she muttered to herself. 'Fred is my brother. Why *can't* I say a simple thing like pregnancy to him? Just because he's a man? I should have asked for Bessie. And they're going to get married whatever we do, so I might as well help!'

The dream continued after she went to bed. Only this time it was compounded by many other factors. Richard Macomber was the central theme, staked out naked over an anthill in the desert, while Beth Murphy, dressed only in a sun-hat and sneakers, leaned over him and poured honey, a drop at a time, down on his sturdy chest.

It was such a delightful dream that she even remembered it as she climbed into the taxi for her morning ride to work. Beth Murphy, dressed only in a hat and sneakers—that was the part that bothered her. 'Some sort of Freudian response,' she muttered to herself as she went by the doorman and into the little lobby. The wind must have been right. She could smell the stale odour of the cafeteria, and marked it down in the corner of her mind as something yet to be done.

The old elevator waited invitingly. She stopped to consider. As she waited the door creaked, half shut itself, and then reopened. 'Oh, no you don't,' she told it, and stalked over to the stairs. Her boss was already in his office when she arrived, out of breath.

'Trouble with the elevator?' he called. She went through. Richard Macomber was relaxing in his deep swivel chair, feet up on the desk, the microphone to a tape recorder in his hand.

'No trouble,' she commented wryly. 'It dared me to get in, so I took the stairs.'

'Coward?'

'A big, yellow stripe down my back. What are you doing?'

'Writing,' he chuckled, and waved the microphone at her. 'What did you expect?'

'I don't know. I've never known an author before. I thought you sat down with some paper and—whatever.' She made an inspection tour around the room. Things were pristine, neat—but not liveable, she told herself. Tomorrow—I mean Monday —flowers.

'Aren't you going to ask me about the baseball practice?'

'This is a business office, after all. I'm being paid to be an executive secretary.'

'I'll tell you about it over lunch,' he called after her.

And, since that fitted in very neatly with her plans, Beth threw him a smile over her shoulder. Mustn't get *too* friendly with him, she warned herself. Nice is all right; friendly is out. At least until after the wedding. It didn't seem all that illogical now that her plan was filled out. Another week to make sure there were no holes in the operation, and our Mr

Macomber will be happy to go to the altar. Well, perhaps not that. He might just balk at a church wedding. She was humming as she started on her second round of research, and was up to her ears in computer paper when he came out.

'Eleven-thirty, lunchtime.' He sang the words in time to samba music, and reached over her shoulder to turn her terminal off when she dallied.

'Oh.' She checked her watch to be sure of the time.

'Doubting Thomasina?'

'What? Oh—no, not exactly. I'm expecting someone to join us for lunch. A man you really need to know. He's usually as punctual as the Naval Observatory Time Signal and—oh, here he is.'

She stood up and came around her desk. The elderly man just coming in the door was a tall oak of a man, with wrists the size of most men's biceps, a proud straight back, and shoulders to match. 'Rudi—Mr Wyskowitz,' she welcomed, adding a little hug that almost cost her a rib. 'This is Mr Macomber.'

The two of them exchanged politenesses. Two big men, warily sizing each other up, while the golden-haired woman watched from the sidelines. In a moment it was 'Rudi' and 'Rich'. Beth heaved a sigh of relief.

'So you've come to have lunch with us?' Macomber asked. The older man looked quizzically at Beth. 'I come because she ask me,' he said. His English was fair, with a strong flavour of the Polish in it.

'Rudi is a consultant. A retired military man,' she hastened to squeeze in. 'He's going to advise us.'

'So? Well, let's go. Where did you book us for lunch?'

'Downstairs,' she reported solemnly, 'in the Macomber Publishing cafeteria.' She latched on to

her purse and shot out of the door, leaving the two
men to follow after her as best they could.

'Hey, wait a minute,' Macomber called. 'In our
cafeteria? I never eat there.'

'Well, seventy per cent of your staff *do*,' she said
grimly.

He shrugged his shoulders and crowded her into
the elevator before she could say a word about the
stairs. Rudi followed, a deep grin playing across his
weather-beaten face.

The smell was gone from the lobby, blown away
by the open doors. The sounds of downtown Boston
rattled in their ears. Pigeons strutted the edge of the
pavement, daring the pedestrians to make them
move.

The men followed her lead down the hall away
from the doors. The smells caught up to them there.
Rudi growled a couple of short, impolite words.
Richard Macomber wrinkled his nose. Beth just
barged ahead. The cafeteria was buzzingly full as
they came in, but the sight of the Big Boss brought
everything to a standstill. Beth led her little expedi-
tion down between the narrow aisles, trailing her
fingers on the table-tops. Behind her, Rudi
Wyskowitz slid a thin, white glove over one hand,
and did the same.

'I can't eat in here,' Macomber protested.

'It gets worse before it gets better,' Beth promised
him. The crowd at the serving tables parted to give
them access. She pointed at the steam tables. 'Now,
you tell me how beans and frankfurters can smell
like cabbage?' she snapped. 'Or that—whatever that
is—roast beef sandwiches? It looks like shoe leather.
And those vegetables! They're not yesterday's left-
overs, they probably came in last week. Or maybe
he buys them as left-overs.'

'I can't face this sort of stuff,' Macomber repeated. 'Let's get out of here.'

Frank Page, the cafeteria manager, came up to the counter. His face fell when he saw Beth. 'Damn,' he roared, 'what are you doing back here?'

'I told you yesterday,' she told him coolly. 'Mr Macomber is upset about this place.'

'Mr Macomber is *very* upset about this place,' Richard added. 'And if I knew what to do about it——'

'Rudi knows what to do,' Beth grinned. 'Twenty-six years a Mess Sergeant in the Marine Corps. Rudi?'

'Close down,' the old man gruffed. 'Shut for over the weekend. Clean, clean, clean. Fans for air circulation. Air conditioners, maybe. It gets hot in Boston. Switch to lunch menu. Put in grills where customers see. Throw out steam tables. Buy better meat. With young people to eat, add milk-shake machines, like that. But first, clean. Paint maybe, too.'

'And what else?' Macomber urged.

'Him.' Rudi pointed across the counter at Page, in his soiled white apron. 'He's gotta go. Today. Right now. Five minutes ago!'

'So do it,' Macomber said.

'Costs money.'

'Spend it. Murphy, give the man an open cheque. God, let's get out of here.'

'Not quite so fast.' Beth caught at the tail of his jacket and he ground to an unwilling stop.

'Now what?' he muttered.

'Make a speech!' He did. Fumbling at first, and then working his way up to an indignant conclusion. All the people in the cafeteria applauded as he led the way out, just behind Mr Frank Page, who was on his way to the unemployment office.

'You're a tough act to follow, Murphy,' Richard

grumbled as they made their way out to the lobby.

'Only doing what an executive secretary is supposed to do,' she said very modestly. 'We don't type letters and send flowers to your girlfriends, you know.'

'I know that,' Macomber returned. '*Now* I know that. Let's go home for lunch.'

'Home?' Dear lord, she thought, I can't take him home. Stacy is still there. I've got to keep the two of them separated until the hook is really set in my fish's mouth! 'No. I can't take you home.'

'But I can take you home with me,' he laughed. Assuming her agreement, he waved an arm. His limousine appeared from nowhere, out from the middle of the double-parked cars, and stopped at the door. Another few minutes brought them to the sea breezes on India Wharf, and the two huge towers that contained his home. Mrs Moore met them at the door.

'And it's good to see you again—Beth,' the housekeeper said. 'I've had my ear talked off about you and your baseball team.'

Althea stuck her head around the corner of a door. 'Miss Beth,' she called, with what might almost have been a friendly tone. She disappeared back into the room behind her before Beth could work up an answer.

Lunch was served in a little nook under the windows, just for the two of them. Mrs Moore hovered for a time, and then disappeared. 'Althea's not eating with us?'

'Not so's you would notice,' he grunted. 'You like this smoked salmon?'

'Love it. But I don't usually have wine at lunch. It makes me very——'

'Interesting?'

'Sleepy. So why is Althea not having lunch? Some

new policy from a stern parent?'

'Not her parent,' he grumbled. 'Her uncle.'

'She's a lovely child,' Beth said very sternly. 'A very much misunderstood child!'

'Is that a fact,' he snorted. 'And how many children do you have, Murphy?'

'You know darn well I don't have any,' she snapped, suddenly angered. 'But that doesn't mean I can't read a great deal on the subject!'

'No, of course not.' She could feel the sarcasm. It thickened the air. And if he asks me one more question like that I'll hit him with the cream bowl, she told herself. He must have seen her gritting her teeth.

'So how was your date with Mac?' he asked nonchalantly.

'With Mac?' She almost gave the game away, but managed to patch things up. 'Oh, with MAC. Last night. Yes.'

'I didn't mean last year. Have some more wine.' She covered the mouth of her glass with one hand.

'No more wine. MAC and I—we had a wonderful time.'

'Took you to some swinging place, did he?'

'Oh, no. Neither of us like that sort of thing. We went to a cosy place with dim lights and soft music, and we—talked back and forth—lord, until past midnight. We're so looking forward to June.'

'I don't want to hear about that,' he snapped.

'Well, you needn't bite my head off,' she answered angrily. 'You showed an interest, so I thought you wanted to know. I was even going to invite you to the wedding!' She clapped her hand over her mouth. *That* was taking things one step too far. It's not nice to tease the lion when you are both inside his cage! Look at him glare. He thinks I'm inviting him to *my* wedding, and when he finds out the invitation is to *his* wedding, he'll really blow his stack!

'I don't think I'll be able to come,' he growled. 'Let's get back to work.'

He was already up and headed for the door when Mrs Moore came in with the ice-cream. The two women looked at each other, shrugged their shoulders, and followed him. Althea stuck her head out of her room again, and waved goodbye.

'When's the next game, Miss Beth?' she called.

'Tomorrow night. Same time, same field. But you can't pitch, you know. Little League rules prohibit a player from pitching more than seven innings a week.'

'I know that. But I play a mean shortstop, too.'

'So they've got you locked up "in durance vile"?'

'No, just in my bedroom.'

'Doing what?'

'You wouldn't believe. Uncle Rich went to the school to talk to the Principal, and they sent me home a load of self-study work I have to do. Is he mean! You can tell *he* was never a little girl!' And with that the child flounced back into her room and closed the door.

'You just take your time, Murphy. I'm sure we've all day.' Beth whirled around to look, startled by the continued anger in his voice. No doubt about it, she thought, measuring the thunder in his eyes, the scars still showing on his face, the tall solid figure of him—this one was certainly never a little girl!

'I'm glad you see the world so happily,' he grumbled as he held the door open. 'Or is it me you think of as being so funny?'

'Oh no,' she squeaked, stuffing the giggles back down her own throat. 'It was—just something that stuck in my—I mean, I wasn't laughing at you.'

She followed him meekly over to the elevator, held on to her stomach as the floor dropped out from under her, and was glad of his steadying hand as they *whished* to a stop. 'It's like being shot through a pneumatic tube,' she gasped.

The idea, or her shaken appearance, seemed to restore his good humour. He held her arm as they went out to the limousine and crawled inside. 'I meant to tell you about your pitchers,' he chuckled. 'That little one, Michael something-or-other——'

'Babson. Michael Babson. He's only nine years old.'

'He wasn't holding the ball right,' he said. 'Once he got the idea, he was a winner. You have the makings of two more fair pitchers, too. I'll check them out tonight. Are you coming?'

'No,' she sighed. 'I have to attend a meeting at Rentasec tonight. The last night of the month. We talk over problems, consider new training programmes—and distribute pay cheques for the month.'

'How long will that take?'

'Very long,' she assured him. 'You know how it is when a bunch of women get together.'

'No, I don't,' Richard laughed. 'I've never been exposed to that sort of party. Maybe I'd better come over and watch after the baseball practice?'

'No,' she gasped. 'No. Only members of the Association are allowed in.' She looked up at him. The glare had gone, and the smile was back. 'We have our secrets, too,' she added.

'I'll bet you do.' A soft rejoinder. Somehow or other he was getting closer. Just at that moment the chauffeur muttered a few short words, twisted the wheel hard, and managed to dodge a driver who had just jumped a stop sign. The sudden movement threw Beth hard up against Richard's shoulder, almost into his lap. His arm came around her in a rescue mission, pulling her solidly against his chest, for some moments after the car had resumed its smooth movements.

'You could let me go now,' she offered tentatively.

'No, I don't think so,' he said absent-mindedly. He was not looking at her, but the fingers that held her shoulder were flexing in and out. 'You didn't fasten your seat-belt. Besides, I like things just the way they are.'

It would be a foolish thing, she told herself, to make a big point about the whole affair. After all, it *was* almost an accident, and I *didn't* have my belt buckled, and it *is* very comfortable here, and I'll think about Stacy tomorrow.

It was so comfortable that she made a vague protest as the car came to a stop and he tried to coax her out. 'Come on, Murphy,' he urged, 'time for work.' She looked up at him, somewhat dazed. It's my lack of sleep, she told herself, not his damn arrogant maleness. But that satisfied look in his eyes said otherwise. There was the male triumphant. Her temper boiled as she struggled, not too gracefully, out on to the pavement.

'I *told* you wine makes me sleepy,' she snapped, and enjoyed watching his face fall, and the conquest signals fade away. So once again they went down a hall, she following him meekly—right into the elevator.

'Oh no,' she wailed, as the door chugged and whuffed in front of her, and gradually closed.

'Don't worry.' He made the announcement as if only women worried in balky elevators. 'I've had it all repaired. It won't stop——' But of course it did. At exactly the same spot, half-way between the second and third floors. 'Damn,' he muttered, moving over to the corner where the trapdoor was located. 'It won't take us a minute to get out.'

'Don't bother on my account,' Beth told him

firmly. 'I have no intention of climbing up that mountain again—I ruined my whole suit the last time.'

'So what do you propose?'

'Push the Emergency button,' she advised. 'I'm going to sit here on the floor and wait to be rescued.'

'That doesn't sound like a bad idea,' he chuckled, and came over beside her. 'Here, sit on my jacket. It gets cleaned on a company expense account.'

'I don't need the Sir Walter Raleigh approach,' She snapped. Having let her pride answer for her, she had to struggle on alone. Sitting down on a bare floor, getting your skirts beneath you, was not all that easy. And the floor was not all that clean. Sidling away from him, she lowered herself gracefully to her knees, swept her skirts under her, and rolled off on to her bottom with her legs tucked up under the skirt.

'Neatly done,' he laughed.

'It just takes practice,' she said firmly. 'The next time I ride in this elevator of yours, I'm going to make sure there's a pillow or a chair inside!'

'Ah, that's it. It's *my* elevator?'

'Of course it's your elevator. Are you denying it?'

'Not at all, firebrand.' He sank to the floor beside her, like some great jungle cat, and dropped an arm over her shoulder. 'And if we follow the logic, my dear. It's my elevator, so I'm responsible for its actions?'

'Right,' she muttered.

'And you're my secretary, so I'm responsible for you, too?'

'Now, wait just a darn minute,' she grumbled. 'That's not the way it—what are you doing?'

'Just accepting my responsibilities,' he murmured in her ear as he pulled her over against him, even closer than they had been in the car. 'Now, isn't that nice?'

'I never practised *that,*' she sighed, grabbing at his wandering hands. He made no move to free them, so finally she relaxed, fell back against his chest, and listened to the world at its work around her, all moving to his heartbeat, just under her ear. It *was* nice. She would never admit it to Richard, but it certainly was. Warm, comforting, pleasant. Nothing moved in the little box that was their world. And time and wine caught up to her. Not worrying about what *his* plans were, she fell fast asleep . . .

CHAPTER SIX

'GOOD lord, Aunt Beth, what are you doing?' Stacy came into the kitchen, looking like some doll in her shorty nightgown, her hair in disarray. Beth sank back on her haunches, blew a wisp of hair out of her eyes, and glanced up.

'I'm washing the floor,' she growled. 'What does it look like I'm doing?'

'It looks like you're beating it to death,' her wise little niece responded. 'Nobody washes floors on their hands and knees any more. Especially on a Saturday morning.'

'Well then, I've just expanded your education,' she snapped. So perhaps I was pounding instead of scrubbing. I can't help it if that man's face keeps glaring up at me from my shiny floor!

It had all started on Friday, when she had come to work roaring mad. After all, it hadn't been *her* fault the damn elevator had jammed. But when a girl wakes up to being rescued, and finds herself lying back against a man she really hates, and there, in front of everybody, he's sitting with a stupid grin on his face, twisting her hair up in little spirals and tying knots in them. Well! And on Friday morning she hadn't had the slightest intention of retracting a single one of the hundreds of words that had poured out of her mouth before her mind was in gear! Not a word. In fact, she had zoomed into Macomber's inner office and repeated a few dozen of them again, just for effect.

There he was, with that same stupid grin on his

face, sitting behind his desk with his feet up. The grin faded very gradually, and when she had finished it was gone—for ever? What a strange way of thinking that was.

'I do believe I've heard this story before,' he grunted. 'I never sit through bad movies twice. Get your pad.' Which left Beth with her eyes open, astonished. Ranting, raving, apologising, any of those she was prepared to face, but not a cold "get your pad".

'I want a complete analysis of the business,' he said when she came back. 'I want to know which divisions are making money and which aren't. I want to know which author sells, and which doesn't. I want to know how our sales compared to last year.'

'By division?'

'By division. Don't interrupt while I'm thinking.'

'Yes sir,' she muttered. And no sir, and three bags full!

'And then I want to know how our expenses compare to last year.'

'Is that all—sir?'

'I think so.' He settled back in his chair and glared at her. She returned the favour. 'That ought to take you the morning at least,' he said complacently, as he reached for the microphone on his dictating machine. 'And in the meantime, I don't want to be bothered. Oh, by the way, was it much trouble undoing the knots?'

Her lips parted again. 'Don't say it,' he warned. She took a second look at him. The scratches on his cheek were fading, but the stitched cut on the other side glared. His heavy eyebrows lined up opposite each other over the ridge of his still-bandaged nose, giving the impression of immense power—or immense evil. Only the hooded dark eyes sparkled a contra-dance. And the corner of his mouth—it kept twitching.

And I'm not falling for that, Beth assured herself fiercely as she went back to her desk. The material he wanted was all there to hand—exactly what she had been researching for the past two days. The phone at her elbow rang.

'I need to see Macomber.' A cool, controlled voice. She fumbled around to place it. Maggie Berman, the Editor-in-Chief.

'He says he's not here,' Beth returned.

'I need at least to talk to him.'

'Nobody talks to Macomber,' sighed Beth. 'But nobody. Something you can't handle? You've been running this place for years, the way I figure it.'

'I don't deny that,' the editor acknowledged. 'But we have this thing. Frank Cranston is the author of our pirate series.' *Is he indeed*, Beth thought. *Well, a lot you know, lady!*

'And?'

'And he's missed his second deadline—as usual. Only Mr Macomber knows how to contact him.'

'I see. And the message is?'

'Get his butt in gear!'

'I'll be sure to tell Mr Macomber if he ever tells me he's back,' Beth chuckled.

'Tell me something, Beth. Is there really a Mr Macomber, or are you running a high-class confidence game up there?'

' "Yes, Virginia, there really is a Santa Claus",' she laughed. 'Why would you doubt it?'

'Oh, I don't know. You do that little secretary game very skilfully. I thought he might have sneaked out on us and gone back to Academe.'

'Gone back where?'

'Academe. He's a college professor, you know. Head of the English Department at some Ivy League place up in Western New York.'

'Cornell,' Beth supplied. Of course, that's why he was up there. That's how Stacy met him. That's the reason—that—that terrible man! She flipped the telephone switch off and sat back in her chair, raging. Ten minutes later, her papers assembled, she knocked perfunctorily on his door and barged in.

'I said nobody——'

'You also said do a management study,' she snapped. 'And here it is.' She dropped the pile of papers in the middle of his desk and glared.

'In—forty-five minutes?' He put down his microphone and thumbed through the papers. 'Well, I'll be damned!'

'Probably,' she muttered. 'Is there anything else?'

'I'm sure there is,' he returned coldly. 'Sit.'

'I'm not your dog,' she retorted, but sat anyway. Macomber made that impression on people. It was easier to do what he commanded rather than argue. But I need to have the last word, she told herself. For my own peace of mind, not for his!

'And I have a message for Frank Cranston,' she barged along. His head came up from the middle of the papers. It wasn't a glare, exactly. It was more like a threat. More like 'I'm going to destroy you, little girl!' She shivered, but ploughed ahead.

'Maggie says to tell Cranston to—let me see now—to "get his butt in gear". That's an exact quote.' Now that the words were out, it all seemed like a very bad idea, baiting the lion. But instead of annihilating her, Richard smiled. Getting through the rest of the day had been like walking on eggs.

And then, that evening, he had turned up at the baseball game, casually dressed, eyes shining, as if there had never been a dispute between them. Only this time he wasn't advising, he was giving orders. A new spirit seemed to ride through the little team.

A new spirit, and ten new aluminium bats, which rang resoundingly all through the game until the lowly Rentasec team had humbled another league leader, ten to one. Beth had restrained her rage—at being displaced by an arrogant male. After all, the boys still cheered *her*. *She* was the manager, and hers the victory.

It was easy to watch him, moving around the field like a wild animal only temporarily caged, and build up her hatred. There had been plenty of reasons on which to base her anger. But it still didn't explain why she had accepted his crazy invitation to go out with him on Sunday, looking for whales to watch! *That* promise had brought her up out of bed too early on Saturday, fully intent on taking out her rage on something inanimate. The kitchen floor had lost.

'Kitchen floors get very dirty very quickly,' she told her niece. 'They need to be scrubbed.'

'Not by me,' Stacy crowed. 'When I marry Roddy I'm going to live in the lap of luxury.'

'Don't give me that, girl. Life doesn't include drinking champagne from your slipper any more. You really mean to marry him?'

The girl dropped down beside her, an anxious look on her face. 'You *did* promise,' she said. It was more a question than an answer.

'Yes,' sighed Beth, scrubbing her way into a corner. 'I promised.' She stood up, her muscles complaining as she moved. 'God, I'm getting old, love. Yes, I promised. It *will* happen.'

'When, Aunt Beth?' The girl was almost jumping up and down in agitation. 'Can I see him?'

'Well now, that's a problem. There are still a couple of little things to be worked out. And it won't be a fancy wedding, you understand. It'll have to be a quiet little affair—a Justice of the Peace, or

something like that. And no, you can't see him. I
need another week to work on the—the scoundrel.
So perhaps the wedding will be ten days from now?'

'I don't mind waiting that long. But I *do* wish I
could see him!'

'That's not on the cards,' Beth returned. 'You'll
see him on the day—no sooner. Then you'll have
the rest of your life to straighten things out. He's
really a rotten man, Stacy. Are you sure?'

'I'm sure,' the girl returned. 'And he's not rotten.
He's just—well—single-minded.'

'You can say that again,' her aunt commented.
But the hug she got lacked nothing, and Beth appre-
ciated that. She hadn't been through a great deal of
hugging lately. Friendly hugging, that is.

She was half-way through the mopping up, when
another thought struck her. 'You know, Stacy, it
might be a good idea for you to go up to Bangor
and visit your Uncle Harold for a few days. See the
children, enjoy the country life, that sort of thing.
How about that?'

It seemed a splendid idea. At least, Stacy liked it,
and it cut down the odd chance that Macomber
might find out where they lived, and come barging
in. So there were two happy Murphy girls waving
goodbye to each other at the Trailways bus terminal
by South Station late that afternoon.

The rest of the day was a hodgepodge for Beth.
There seemed hardly any reason to cook a meal for
one. She made a ham sandwich, and carried it
downstairs with her, where MAC waited, humming
away in its corner. There was plenty of work to be
done, and half a dozen letters which Mary had not
quite got through. She chomped her way through it
all, then wandered back upstairs.

There was nothing worth watching on TV, so
Beth activated her video recorder and spent an hour

with *Mrs Miniver*, the old black and white tear-jerker. And so to bed.

Sunday morning came in like a perfect charmer. The sun rose on the harbour islands, and tiptoed into her flat like an old friend. Beth bounced out of bed to face the challenge of life, and almost crawled back under the sheets when she remembered what she had promised.

There was an eight o'clock Mass, whose calming effect settled her down. What do you wear for a day of whale-watching? Unsure of herself, she changed out of her simple dress into a pair of beige cord slacks, a light blouse, and a big straw hat. There was plenty of sun-screen in her bag, her hair was neat—and she wasn't ready to go. What did he expect to have happen? Swimming?

Just to make sure, she stripped, donned her best bikini, tucked her briefs and bra into her bag, and fumbled around for sun-glasses. The clock was coming up on nine, and she had promised him a nine-thirty meeting. Shrugging her shoulders, she telephoned for a cab. After all, it was *almost* business, and she had no qualms about charging it to his account.

She was still unsure of herself when the cab dropped her off in front of his building. She checked her clothing, settled her hat, and squirmed out. Richard Macomber was waiting outside for her, dressed in slacks and shirt, dark glasses, and a big grin. The bandage was off his nose. He was beginning to look what he was, she thought, a very successful young man. A very successful, *big* young man. He snatched her beach bag away from her, took her elbow, and headed her down the wharf towards the water.

'I brought the boat around early,' he said. She

was having trouble keeping up with him, and that
iron hand would not let go.

'Where's Althea?' she gasped.

'Althea?'

'Yes, you know. Your niece Althea.'

'Oh, that one.' He laughed down at her. 'She
hates whales. And boats too, for that matter. She's
gone out to her grandmother's in Lexington for the
day.'

They were at the foot of the wharf. She could see
the oily water lapping at the pilings. The boat was
tied up by the landing, and there was not a soul in
sight. A shiver went down her spine.

'I—wait a minute,' she protested. 'I thought
—we're going out in that thing just by ourselves?'

'Of course. What did you expect?'

'I expected company,' she said slowly. 'I didn't
expect to have to spend the day——'

'Fending me off?' Richard's smile was enough to
send her alarm system into convolutions. 'You don't
have to worry about that, Murphy. Look at the size
of that thing. Somebody's got to steer, you know.'

'Do I?' She looked down at the boat. It was not
at all what she had expected. A good thirty feet
long, it boasted a double cabin, mahogany-work
topside, a flying bridge, and a shaded afterdeck big
enough to hold an orgy! Now why did I think of
that word? she asked herself as he tugged her down
on to the landing-stage, and helped her up over the
side on to the boat. Why orgy?

'It's a pretty big boat,' she observed as she strove
to catch her breath. 'Are you sure you can handle it
single-handed?'

'Easy,' he returned. 'And besides, I've got you.'

'No, you haven't got me!' she insisted deter-
minedly.

'I mean as an assistant, Murphy.'

'I don't think that's very funny,' she snapped.

'No, it certainly isn't.' He was all seriousness. A frown flashed across his face and was gone. He was working at a line up at the bow, freeing it from the little brass bracket that held it.

'I'm—not sure I really want to go,' she insisted. 'I might get seasick or something.'

'Indeed you might. Come on.' He led her up two sets of ladders to the flying bridge, where they could stand out in the open air, yet be protected from spray by the glass windscreen. He pushed a button, and the boat began to throb. He advanced the double throttles. The pier began to slide away behind them, very slowly.

'I'm *sure* I don't want to go,' Beth stated mutinously.

'I can see that,' he returned, advancing the throttles. The craft came up at the bow and began hurrying towards the harbour islands, skipping slightly from side to side as it met the incoming swells from the ocean.

'You're not listening to me!' she shouted, trying to make herself heard over the roar of the engine. Richard was measuring the gap ahead of them, between Deer Island on the north and Long Island, to the south. Boston Light was dead ahead, marking the channel. She tugged at his arm.

'You're not listening to me,' she repeated.

He turned around and grinned. 'Oh, I'm listening, but I'm not paying any attention. An old Yankee trait.'

'Well, I never did trust any old Yankees,' she shouted back. 'I'm not going!'

'OK. I can slow down if this tanker behind us keeps clear. Do you want to get off now?'

'Ohhh! You're an—impossible—man!'

'I've heard that said. If you're not getting off, why

don't you sit down and relax? And don't forget to
put on your sun-screen. There's a tremendous reflec-
tion off the water on such a sunny day.'

There was hardly anything else to do. The boat
was running fast and free, kicking up a bow wave
that sent showers back across the main deck. Beth
watched as they roared past the two outer islands,
where old Fort Standish and equally old Fort Warren
pointed their empty gun-ports at the sea. Above
them a pair of seagulls tracked them, as they did
every ship, waiting for rubbish to be thrown off the
fan-tail. Beth wandered around the pointed shape of
the bridge and absorbed everything as the breeze
toyed with her hat.

Clear of the islands the swell in Massachusetts
Bay began to rock them. Ahead, for however many
miles there were, was England. She was giggling at
the thought when Richard swung the wheel and they
turned away from the main shipping channel and
headed for the tip of Cape Cod, seen hazily in the
distance.

'Where are we going?' She had walked full circle
around the deck, and now was back at his ear. He
pointed straight ahead.

'We'll clear Provincetown,' he yelled, 'then go out
to Stellwagon Shoals. That's where the whales will
be, if there are any.'

'If there are any? You mean we're going all the
way out there in the *hope* there might be whales to
watch?'

'Don't be sarcastic, Beth. It's not nice. Did you
expect we have an appointment with the whales?
They'll come if they've a mind to, and not otherwise.'

'Boy,' she sighed, disgusted. The boat roared on.

'You could use a sun-tan,' he suggested. 'Why
don't you slip off that blouse and get more exposure?'

'What do you think I am,' she snapped, 'a free peep-show?'

'If I told you what I think, you wouldn't like it,' he assured her. 'Do you really want to know?'

'No, I don't,' she admitted hesitantly. 'And I don't tan. Not all the girls in the world turn a beautiful butter-brown, you know. Some of us just burn. If you wanted baked goods, you should have asked one of your other—one of your playmates along.'

'Maybe I should have,' he sighed, and went back to his navigational problems.

She looked at his wide, strong back, fighting against the strange wishes that haunted her, and gave up. The ladder that led down to the day cabin was a little hard to handle, now they were out in the bay. She inched her way carefully down, and went inside.

The door closed out the roar of the wind, and muted the song of the engines. The cabin was a sensuous delight. Bright with light colours, sunshine coming in through its serried windows, the carpeted floor absorbed her footprints and sprang up again. Forward were the navigational aids—a sheltered wheel, radio, and duplicates of the controls up on the flying bridge. The room was surrounded by a soft-cushioned bench that shaped a letter U, with the hatch to the lower cabin in its mouth.

She flipped open the hatch cover and went down into the hull. Around an open centre were three rooms. Two contained beds, the other was the ship's head. Beth tested one of the beds by the tried and true method—letting herself fall into it. It bounced her gently a couple of times, and then welcomed her.

'So this is how the idle rich live,' she muttered, curling up into a ball. Her hat had been left in the day cabin; now her hair came down loose around her shoulders. The boat maintained its rhythmic movement, and her lack of sleep the previous night caught up with her. Stifling a yawn, she sprawled out on her back, legs outflung, ran a finger through her hair, and slipped off.

The dream came after some time. A dream that brought a smile to her lips, and caused her to squirm in the bed. Macomber was in it, but in the half-world of dreams she felt no inhibitions, no hate. His cool hand caressed her cheek, wandered in her hair, touched her ears. The fingers dropped lower, unbuttoning her blouse and gently laying it aside. She could feel the rise of passion as he toyed with the bra of her bikini, then flicked it aside to let her generous breasts stand of their own strength.

Softly his head came down over her, until his lips closed on the hardened peak before him. Teasing, gentle, hard, demanding, her passions cycled under the pressure, her body tossed, and his hand slipped lower, to the zipper of her cords.

In a world of many noises, there was no logical reason why such a small sound should awaken her, but it did. Beth came up out of her dreams, dazed, struggling not to awaken, yet driven to open her eyes.

His head was there, just as she dreamed, his tongue busy at the honey of her, his hand slipping between her thighs in gentle pursuit of the mystery of it all. For a moment she lay still, her hand moving to his head, holding him. And then the import of it all penetrated.

'My God!' she screamed at him. 'What are you doing?'

He lifted his head and stared at her, his eyes large and glazed. 'You have to ask?'

She struggled to push him away. He resisted her silent struggle. She began to moan, from the desperation of it all. It was the noise, rather than her strength, that pushed him away.

He sat up on the edge of the bed, feet on the floor. 'Now what does all *that* mean?' he asked. 'You surely knew what to expect when I invited you out?'

'Think what you want,' she cried, tears beyond recall. 'Just—leave me alone, damn you. Isn't one Murphy enough for you?'

'I don't know what you're talking about, and I surely don't want you to explain,' he sighed. 'Here. Let me help.'

His capable fingers pushed her fumbling hands aside, and dressed her as if she were a little girl. 'Come on. So it shouldn't *all* be lost, let's go look at the whales.' He extended his hand, but she flinched away from it. Another thought had struck her. 'Who—who's sailing the boat?' There was a gleam of terror in the back of her eyes.

'Automatic pilot,' he grunted. 'Come on. You're a barrel of fun down here. I don't think I could take another minute.' He ushered her back up to the flying bridge, with one hand in the small of her back, and then went back to the cabin. It gave her time to put her dominoes back up in line. She smoothed down her blouse, checked the zipper of her slacks, and threw her head back.

The clear ocean wind snatched her hair, twirling it all behind her like a golden cloud. The smell of it cleansed her mind. There were a few high-flying gulls overhead, their shrill call echoing over the quiet ocean. Land was but a shadow behind them. The boat was hardly making headway through a green ocean. And he was back again, swinging a picnic basket.

She eyed Macomber nervously, not sure of anything any more. He paid her no attention, but

rather went over to the side of the coaming and let
down a suspended table. 'Come on,' he called.
'Coffee. Sandwiches. Not the Ritz, but it will have
to do.'

'I—are the whales nearby?' Beth managed, sidling
carefully in his direction.

'As you see——' he gestured towards the water
'—we're over the shoals. If they're coming, this is
where they'll show.'

'How can you tell where we are?'

'Water colour,' he grunted as he poured two half-
cups of coffee. 'Milk?' She shook her head. 'Deep
ocean waters are blue,' he explained. 'Shoal water
shows green. We're right in the middle of the Gulf
Stream. Drink up.'

She took the proffered cup, glad of its warmth,
and treasured it between her hands. It gave her more
than warmth. It gave her courage. She swallowed,
sipped, and the world seemed sunnier again.

'Good coffee,' she offered hesitantly.

'What else? Mrs Moore makes everything good.'

'That's not—not very nice. I'm—trying to make
conversation, and you just——'

'I know. I just act like a sore loser, don't I?' That
grin was back. She felt instant relief. 'Nibble on a
sandwich.' He offered her a neatly cut half, with
ham peering out at her.

'We—seem to be on a single track,' she said
nervously. 'I had a ham sandwich for supper last
night, too.'

'OK,' he chuckled. 'Pax?'

'I don't know what you—oh—yes. Pax.'

She bit deeply into the sandwich, and washed it
down with a gulp of black coffee. It could hardly be
called a decent swallow. His hand slammed her on
the back. 'There,' he shouted, 'it blows!' Beth almost
choked, and half screamed. Directly alongside the

boat a huge form came straight up out of the water, hung there for a moment, with the sun gleaming off its black uppersides and its white underside, and then splashed back, all forty feet of it, with a smash that sprayed the boat from stem to stern, and rocked it madly.

She dropped her coffee-cup, looked for something to hang on to, and found only Richard Macomber. In a moment of terror, he would have to do, she told herself fiercely, and hung on. 'What?' she spluttered.

'A humpback whale,' he shouted at her, tugging her over to the coaming. 'A beauty. Did you see that?' He was overflowing with enthusiasm. So much that it carried her along, too. 'Look. A whole school of them!'

She craned her head to see a half-dozen of the huge shapes playing escort to them, ploughing through the water with their backs and wakes visible, an occasional tail fin coming up above water to move them along.

'What are they doing?' she yelled, amazed at the size of the creatures.

'Feeding,' he returned. 'They come north along the Gulf Stream, on their way to Greenland—and maybe even the Arctic Ocean. See those bubbles? Watch. There's a whale down deep, beneath a school of fish. He's blowing bubbles at the fish to herd them together, and then he'll—here he comes!'

And here he *did* come, cutting through the surface at full speed, vaulting into the air with his mouth slowly closing on his meal, only to fall back again with that tremendous splash that shook the world.

'How—how big was that?' Beth was having trouble breathing in the face of this great mystery of the sea.

'Not too big,' he told her. 'About fifty feet, maybe.

Say about forty-five tons. Something in that order.
Look at that little fellow! There are calves in the
school. No wonder they're going so slowly.'

'Babies?' she queried.

'Yes, of course. The whale is a mammal.'

'I know that. They might even have come ashore
at some time in the development of their species,
and then gone back into the sea.'

'Great education,' he chuckled.

'*Encyclopaedia Britannica,* 1946,' she returned
pertly. 'How did you know it was a humpback
whale? I thought they were almost extinct.'

'You just look at them, Murphy. They have a
hump on their back just in front of the dorsal fins.
And yes, they were almost extinct. But hunting
whales is gradually being outlawed. And besides, the
humpback doesn't have the oil that a big sperm
whale carries. But I guess that's all the show we're
going to get.' He looked up at the sun, now half-
way down in the west. 'And we'd better get going.
The weatherman promises rain for tonight and
tomorrow.'

He moved forward on the bridge, engaging the
throttles, and gradually turning the boat into the
wind. Ahead of them now there were one or two
spurts of water as the whales cleared their breathing
passages after a deep dive, and then the bow of the
boat curved away from them, pointing back towards
the smudge on the horizon that was Boston, and the
speed picked up.

There had been something about the watching,
the curiosity, the playfulness of these, the largest
mammals on earth, that relaxed Beth, and blocked
out all the other happenings of the day. She stood
close beside him, feeling the strength of his arm
around her shoulders as he steered one-handed,
occasionally squeezing her in a companionable way.

'I'm sorry we misunderstood each other,' he said quietly. She kept looking straight ahead, afraid of what her face might show should she turn towards him. He's a dangerous man, she thought, but was unwilling to fight against him for this brief time.

The sun was glittering from behind the glass of the high-rise buildings of downtown Boston, spattering drops of colour off the Hancock building, the Kennedy building, the Federal Reserve building. Below the sun, a long line of low, black clouds blotted out Cambridge and the west. The bay was providing them with cross-chops, little flickers of wind that heralded the coming storm, causing the boat to pitch and yaw at the same time. She neglected it all, and stood side by side with the man. He was not the same man she had known all week. That one was a mad mixture of businessman and playboy. This one was all man, strong, capable, feeling. He made her proud to be where she was, who she was, and what she was. Proud that she was a woman.

CHAPTER SEVEN

SHE was late for work on Monday morning. It had nothing to do with the horrendous rush-hour that crushes the spirit in Boston on a work day. It had nothing to do with the drizzle that washed the air. It had everything to do with the Sunday spent in the ocean air and happiness. And perhaps just a touch to do with the six hours Beth had spent with MAC, her multiple access computer, slaving to catch up on the week's postings, and the future's guidance. In any event, the building was bustling when she splashed into the lobby at ten o'clock.

'A little wet?' Sam, the doorman, helped her out of her plastic raincoat.

'More inside than out,' she grinned. 'I don't know why I don't get a real raincoat. This thing, especially in the summer, makes you perspire more than can possibly rain on you!'

He returned the grin as he shook her coat, folded it neatly and handed it back. 'Was a nice spring,' he said wistfully. And it's a nice summer, she thought. All of Boston's springtime promise had come true. In her tiny back yard the wistaria had blossomed and fled, to be replaced by the roses scrambling up the side of the porch along their rambling vines. 'Oops, I'm late!' She snapped herself out of her musings, and dashed for the stairs. The elevator door rattled as she went by, in a sort of invitation.

'Not me,' she muttered as she rushed by. 'Twice is enough. You don't have to hit *me* with a brick to convince me.' The elevator sighed, crashed its door shut, and wandered upward to a summons.

Beth was still smiling as she raced up the stairs, two at a time, but was out of breath when she tumbled into her own office and hung her rain things on the old-fashioned coat-rack. Her plastic hood had done little good for her hair. It was down around her face, having fallen out of the tight bun she usually arranged at the nape of her neck. She fretted at it with a finger, but left it in order to water her plants.

Housekeeping done, Beth smoothed down her hair, rearranged her blouse, twitched her navy-blue skirt around, and went into the inner office. 'Hi,' Macomber called. His feet came clumping down off the desk, and he laid his microphone aside. 'For a minute there I thought you weren't coming. But it *did* give me the chance to finish the book. A day on the salt water was too much for you, I suppose?'

'I'm terribly sorry,' she said, doing her usual inspection sweep of his office. 'I was up so darn late last night with MAC that I——' She stopped short in the middle of the sentence. The smile was gone from his face, and she could see the blood rising. Beth took a step or two backwards, overwhelmed by the angry glare. His fist slammed down on the top of his desk.

'And you just couldn't wait to tell me,' he snarled. 'You spend the day with me and the night with him? Great!'

'I don't know what you're talking about,' she returned as fiercely as she could. 'I—what business is it of yours who I spend my nights with?'

'But you *did* spend the night with Mac, didn't you?' He wasn't waiting for an answer, so she offered none. 'The whole night, I suppose. Is he as good in bed as he is out, I wonder? Of course, it's June, and wedding bells, and all that. A white wedding, or do you plan to display the truth?'

'It's none of your damn business,' she spat back at him. 'Just because you hire me for a day's work doesn't mean I'm accountable to you for—oh hell!' The tears came like super-drops from thunder clouds, and the tiny handkerchief she carried could do nothing to still them.

'Don't give me the weeps,' he snarled. 'I'm really not interested in your lovers, just in a day's work. Shall we get to it?'

Another rhetorical question, of course. He had already come to his conclusions, and Beth wanted no part of trying to sway him. Not now. Surge after surge of anger swelled up in her. And poor Stacy wants to marry this clod, she thought. It would serve him right! She sniffed back the last few tears and took her pen out of her pocket. 'I'm ready whenever you are,' she said coldly.

He slumped back in his chair, looking as if he had suffered a defeat of tremendous proportion. On the desk in front of him were all the papers and graphs she had compiled the week before. 'This is all accurate?' The suspicion rode the words into the ground.

'The figures come from your own computer,' she returned. 'As far as your memory banks can be trusted, yes, those are accurate.'

'And just what are you telling me?'

'I'm not telling you anything,' she sighed. 'Your computer is saying that the Detective Division is making a good profit, except for one line of books which, according to the graph, has died on the market. The Romance Division is steadily losing ground. Your authors are not keeping up with the times. The Adventure-Spy Division is in excellent shape. And the Biography Division is losing money hand over fist.'

'Hah!'

'Did you want me to write that down?'

'Don't give me your prim little sarcasms, Murphy. Why is Biography losing so much money?'

'How would I know? That's for your Editor to explain. I can tell you, though, that they are insisting on extra-fine covers, expensive binding work, fancy type. The average cost per book has gone up over the last three years by twenty-seven per cent. Why don't you ask your questions at the next board meeting?'

'What a wonderful suggestion,' he commented, his voice dripping with sarcasm. 'And what's this?'

This was a graph, showing a steadily declining line. 'Dorothy Maincliffe,' she offered, looking over her shoulder. 'Our records show she's eighty years old, and I suspect she's outlived her prime audience.'

'Yes,' he sighed, 'but you wouldn't understand. She and my father were beaux in the twenties. Strangely enough, they both married other people. But you know how it is with first loves.

'No, I don't,' she grated. 'You intend to carry her because your father is still in love with her?'

'Exactly, Murphy. Something you wouldn't understand. The Macombers are famous for clinging to their first true love.'

'Yeah, I'll bet,' she muttered. 'You've got a track record to prove it, haven't you?'

'What did you say?'

'Nothing. I—I was just thinking about what to have for supper tonight.'

'Another night with Mac, I suppose.'

She glared back at him. I really could hate you, she thought, I really could! 'Probably,' she answered. She had been battered around emotionally too much for one morning, and a soft answer turneth away wrath—wasn't that the way the saying goes? 'May I go now?'

'Yes, you can go now,' he almost shouted at her. And then, as they both stood up, he said very softly, 'I've finished my book, Murphy. From now on *I'll* run Macomber Publishing.'

'What a happy thought,' she told him grimly. 'I'll be sure to pass the word.' She slammed out of his office, never looking back. The rest of the day was anti-climactic. Everyone who called for Macomber was immediately put through. Everyone who visited was immediately announced. And, in between, Beth finished up the pile of letters and internal bulletins which had been lying around for the past week or more.

At noon he swept out of his office, every inch the Roman legate. 'Lunch,' he announced. 'Come.' She shrugged, scrabbled around for her bag, and followed in his wake. He went to the elevator—she detoured to the stairs. Four floors down, and she was in the lobby seconds before he arrived. Follow-the-leader again, moving along behind his broad, strong back, thinking thoughts that ran from murder to seduction, and in no particular order. Into the company cafeteria.

New lights in the ceiling had banished all the gloom. There was an odour—flowers. The long mess-hall tables were gone, replaced by neat little four-person units. Each table had its own vase, its own flowers. A fan rumbled in the background, refreshing the air. The steam tables were gone, replaced by a grill, a sandwich counter, and a fountain. Behind the serving counter two neatly dressed women handled the food, and behind them, Rudi Wyskowitz proudly officiated. There was a scattering of applause as they came in. The tables were full.

'Staggered hours,' Rudi explained in his rumbling

voice. 'Nicer. Can take time to eat and talk, and not get ulcers. Nice place.'

Beth hardly knew what she was eating. The food was good, but the transformation was overwhelming. And across the table from her Macomber was very slowly winking one eye at her. 'Everybody loves the boss,' he half whispered. 'What a good man I am!'

She almost choked on her sandwich, and had quick recourse to her coffee to wash her throat out.

'You were saying?'

'I was about to say "yes",' Beth returned, coughing. 'I didn't realise that modesty was one of your great attributes.'

'Runs in the family,' he announced in lordly fashion. Had it not been for the twinkle in his eye she might have believed him.

By the end of the day she had cleared up most of the left-over work. He was still cloistered in his office, having called for, in succession, the senior editors of each division. Each of them had come out wiping their brows, so to speak. The Editor-in-Chief was sharing the inquisition when Beth finally decided to pack it in, and go home.

Naturally, with the rain and all, taxis were hard to find. She was half soaked by the time she succeeded, and the driver grumbled at having to leave the Financial Section of the city to go all the way over to South Boston. Which is not, as everyone knows, actually south of the city centre, but more nearly to the east. The driver continued to grumble at the size of the tip she left him, but Beth was sick to death of people who wanted tips for poor service. She fought her way up the front steps, swept by a wind coming in off Pleasure Bay, and thankfully tucked herself in for the night.

Tuesday was some small improvement. The sun

shone. Macomber was still playing lord of the manor, with department heads and project managers all taking their place in the line, waiting for his interrogation. Only one item broke the flow of the day. At about ten-thirty Beth received a call from the company nurse.

'For insurance purposes,' that lady explained, 'everyone has to have a physical, even temporary workers. And today's the day the doctor is here.'

'But I'm not really a temporary worker,' she protested. 'I'm employed by Rentasec, and am only here on a contract basis.'

The argument looked as if it might be long—and not worth the bother—so she picked up her bag and went down to the third floor. For a temporary affair, the examination was more detailed than she had been exposed to for many a moon. And in the end the nurse whipped out the longest needle Beth had ever seen, and threatened her with it.

'Blood,' the doctor explained.

'I'm—afraid of needles,' she quavered.

'It won't hurt a bit.'

'What you mean is that it won't hurt *you* a bit. How about me?'

'I guarantee it won't hurt *you,* either,' the doctor laughed. 'Whatever happened to the courage of the Murphys?'

'My brothers have all *that* blood,' she sighed. 'I just have the cowardly stuff.' But it all seemed inevitable, and she submitted, even though the doctor had lied.

The idea bothered her all through the rest of the day. Why would anyone in the publishing house worry about *her* health? It still bothered her when she shut down her terminal at just three o'clock, and headed home for the Little League game. Not ten minutes after she arrived on the field a long grey limousine drove up, and the two Macombers climbed out.

'Am I going to play, Miss Beth?' Althea, with her face anxiously turned up, wishing with her eyes.

'You're here,' Beth chuckled, 'so you *have* to play. The league rules require that every member of a team must play through at least one inning at bat. So I think—you'll pitch?'

The girl grabbed up her glove and went yelling out into the infield practice, stuffing her hair up under her cap as she went. A few of the early fans applauded, and the boys on the team offered a variety of cat-calls and whistles and whipped the ball at her full speed, as if she were just another boy.

'No doubt about it,' said Beth over her shoulder. 'This team has confidence these days.'

'No doubt about it,' the deep voice behind her chuckled. She whirled around, to find her nose buried in the chest of Richard Macomber. And he was smiling.

'I—I didn't think you'd come,' she said softly.

'Because I've been a bear?'

'I—yes.'

'Well, that doesn't lose me my job as assistant coach, does it? I like baseball.'

'You must have played well when you were younger. It's too bad you didn't catch on in the professional league, but we appreciate your skill—Mr—er—Richard.'

'It was fun while it lasted,' he chuckled.

'And that's when you decided to be a teacher?'

'Not that easy, woman. I flunked out of baseball, then tried Hollywood.'

'Oh my!'

'And flunked out of that. So I thought to become a writer.'

'And became an instant success, didn't you?'

'Oh sure.' He ruffled her hair with one friendly hand, doing just what the wind was doing, but causing her to tremble just the slightest. 'Every author is an instant success, lady. I almost starved to death. *That's* when I decided to be a school-teacher. To support myself while I learned how to write.'

'And then?'

'And then my cowardly father decided to give up on Macomber Publishing, and retire suddenly. So here I am.'

'You—you did very well today.'

'And that cost you a lot to say, didn't it!' He was grinning down at her, just as an eddy of wind picked up a little brick-dust and sprayed her ochre, and the umpire came over, grumbling about not having her line-up card. She blinked her eyes clear. He was still grinning. She turned her back to get away from those clear dark eyes, and filled out the card.

There were more fans in the stands. The word was spreading that Rentasec had finally discovered how to play the game. And while Beth was urging her batters on, Macomber was behind the stands illustrating to the infielders how you block a ground ball, rather than let it roll through your legs. Beth was not the least bit surprised when her team won, fourteen to one. A number of parents stopped by the dug-out to congratulate her, and when they had left, the Macombers were gone, too.

Wednesday and Thursday went slowly. Action had dropped off in the executive suite. 'I'm not available,' Macomber grunted when he came in on Friday. 'I have to do some thinking.' So she barred the door.

'He's hibernating?' asked Maggie Berman, the Editor-in-Chief, on the telephone.

'Well, he said thinking,' Beth returned. 'And I don't hear any noises from inside.'

'Well, I just wanted to tell him we've received the first ten chapters of the new Frank Cranston book. Quite a surprise. Different.'

'Oh. That's nice.'

'You're not a fan?'

'Can't stand the stuff,' Beth sighed. 'But then I'm not noted for my art appreciation. And it's my last day.'

'Your last day, Beth? That can't be. We need you badly.'

'That's how you've got me—badly,' Beth quipped. 'But Grace What's-her-name will be back on Monday, and I'll be out on some other temporary job. I *have* enjoyed it, though. All of it. I think.'

She hung up with regret. It *had* all been fun. All but the reason for her being here at all. With Maggie's thanks and congratulations still ringing in her ear, Beth went over to the window and stared. The Customs House tower was right in front of her, but she didn't see it. Her mind was on the telephone call she had received from Stacy on Thursday night.

'I'm on pins and needles, Aunt Beth. Is everything arranged?'

'Not yet, love. Just a few more days. Don't worry. Are you having a good time?'

'Fantastic, Aunt Beth. There's this boy next door—well, he's really a man. He does radio broadcasts, and *is* he cute!'

'I'll bet he is,' Beth responded. 'Well, not to worry. Come back before Wednesday morning, will you?'

'OK.'

There was just a hint of disappointment in the word and, for a second, Beth doubted the whole basis of her scheme. Stacy was so damn volatile, and you could hardly be sure whether she wanted to marry Roddy or not. Her aunt was confused by the whole affair.

'But I really love Roddy,' the girl said before she hung up. And that was it. Beth came in to work determined to set the last phase of the plan in motion.

'Lunch,' said Macomber as he emerged from his office at noon. 'Hey, it's getting cloudy. Do we play in the rain?'

'No,' Beth told him. 'The weather forecast is for heavy rains. Our field is newly overhauled, and the League doesn't want us out there chewing it up in wet weather. The Secretary notified me about ten minutes ago that all games are cancelled.'

'Too bad. How about eating?'

'I—I can't today. There's something I have to do.'

'You're sure?'

'Positive.' And please don't ask me what it is, she thought. He waffled, as if planning to ask just that, then finally decided to go on by himself. Beth had been holding her breath all that time. When the door closed behind him she exhaled one huge sigh of relief.

She went to the door and locked it. Both telephone answering machines came on as she pushed the appropriate button. The little loose-leaf booklet was still in the top drawer of her desk. She pulled it out and laid it flat in front of her. Eighteen pages of instruction on how to lock or unlock the various segments of the system. A code book, complete in itself. It was the last two pages she wanted. How to change the code words that did the actual locking. She studied the sheet for a moment, then carefully edged it out of the book and stuffed it in her bag.

Rich Macomber was back at two o'clock. 'Coming down like a river,' he commented as he shook himself. Like a great big wonderful dog, Beth thought. Wonderful. If it wasn't for Stacy, I'd—but Stacy was a fact of life, and no amount of dreaming would change a minute of it. She offered him a bleak smile, hoping that what she felt would not show on her usually mobile face.

He came over to her desk, making himself at home by resting a hip on it. 'Last day, Murphy.' Not a question, but rather a sad statement. 'We're going to miss you around here.'

'Who knows, perhaps somebody in the organisation will need a secretary some time,' she offered hopefully.

'Perhaps. But—say, with your baseball game rained out, you must have a free evening. Why don't we go out on the town?'

'I'm really sorry,' she told him, 'but I—I have an engagement for this evening.' It wasn't quite untrue. She wasn't free. There was still all that mass of work waiting for her at Rentasec.

'Oh God,' he groaned. 'Mac again?'

She sat up straight in her chair, ready to fight. 'Yes, Mac again. It's always Mac.'

'You plan to spend the rest of your life with that no-good?'

'You don't know him at all,' she snapped. 'What gives you the right to make judgements? And if I want to spend the rest of my life with him, what's to stop me?'

He held up both his hands in surrender. 'OK, OK.' His face was sombre, tired. 'I know. It's a case of being an hour late and a dollar short, isn't it?'

'I haven't any idea what you're talking about, Mr Macomber.'

'Oh my! Have we gone *that* far back? *Mr* Macomber?' She ducked her head, refusing to meet his eyes. She could see the toe of his shoe swinging back and forth. Then he muttered something unintelligible, and stood up. 'Well, it's terrible weather—you've done a fine job—I can't tell you how much I've enjoyed working with you, Beth. Mac is a lucky fellow. I wish you both every happiness. You can go along home now. There's no sense sitting around here on a Friday afternoon. I have to go out myself.'

'I—I could stay until five,' she said in a tentative small voice. 'Where are you going?'

'Go along home,' he sighed, 'there's a good girl. I think I'll go out and get drunk.' He put his raincoat back on, leaned over and kissed her gently on the forehead, and walked out.

Walked out of my life, Beth told herself. I—Stacy needs him. But deep inside her there was a little ball of pain that gnawed at her all the way home. She bustled around her apartment doing housework, showered, pecked at her dinner, and went downstairs to MAC, to work her way through the accumulation of things that needed to be done.

'If only you knew what a problem you are,' she told the machine at twelve o'clock. 'I could kick you, but it wouldn't do any good, would it? I really wish——' But then one doesn't get to be a trusted aunt by succumbing to all the wishes in the world. What was that phrase—'If wishes were horses, beggars would ride'? The words echoed around the empty room. The thought haunted her as she dragged herself upstairs.

There was one more task to perform. She tried three times to dial directly to her brother Fred's house in California, but her finger slipped in the dialling. She finally stuck her finger in the O hole, and called for operator assistance.

'Fred?'

'Beth? Are we running a coast-to-coast Murphy

service? This makes three times you've called me in the last week.'

'Well—I can afford it. How's everybody?'

'Everybody's fine. Can I speak to my daughter?'

'Not from here, Fred. She's gone up to visit Harold for a few days.'

'Speak up, Beth, I can hardly hear you. We must have a bad line.'

'No, there's nothing wrong with the line. I—I'm just tired. I wanted you to know that—that everything's going along fine.'

'That's good. You could have mailed a letter for twenty-six cents.'

'I suppose. But—I wanted to hear your voice.'

'What is it, Beth? I can hear trouble in your voice.'

'I—it's just a cold. You know how I am with summer colds. Is there anything new in the strike at Halmen Software?'

'Funny you should ask,' he chuckled. 'Yes, there's something new. The whole place burned down last night. Arson, the police are saying. Why are you so interested in a small software company?'

'I—I just have an interest. Everything burned?'

'Everything. Lost all of their files, and half the building. They'll be months getting things straight with their customers.'

Beth sighed. It was just the news she wanted to hear, but somehow it bothered her. 'Thanks, Fred,' she said, and carefully hung up. The paper was in her bag. She took it out and flattened it on the kitchen table. 'Halmen Software', its inscription read. 'The following instructions allow user organisations to change the LOCK/UNLOCK code-words at their discretion. In case problems arise, call Halmen Software free of charge, at 1-800-SOFTWARE.' Beth used her apron to dry the tear that had fallen on the page, and began to study the problem.

Saturday morning dawned with drizzle and fog.
A small tropical storm was moving up the Atlantic
coast towards New England and these clouds were
its outriders. The cleaning crews were scheduled at
Macomber at eight o'clock on Saturdays. At nine
Beth drove up in a cab, and walked into the lobby.
She still had the identification badge that all
employees wore. The doorman was not Sam; she
passed him by—and the elevator as well. A crew of
three were at work in the executive suite. She sat
patiently at her desk until they had finished, then
activated her computer terminal. It took her an
hour, going over the instructions step by step, to
change every one of the computer LOCK code-
words. When she had finished, no one but herself
could make use of the computer for any purpose,
and only she had the instructions that would allow
anyone else to change the code-words to something
else.

'There,' she muttered as she gave the final key a
stroke, and watched while the machine locked itself
up. 'And that'll throw something into the fan!'

'What did you say, dearie?' The elderly woman
with the mop was standing patiently by, waiting for
her to leave.

'Oh, nothing,' she sighed. 'I just said that's the
way to finish up the plan.'

'Probably,' the woman returned. Beth got out of
the way and walked carefully down the four flights
of stairs. Her eyes just would not focus. She cried
all Saturday afternoon, and then ordered for a pizza
to be delivered, settling down with MAC for the rest
of the weekend. The machine was cold comfort.

CHAPTER EIGHT

THE WAITING was the hardest thing Beth had ever done. She sat through Monday and Tuesday in a daze, never going more than ten feet from a telephone. 'Something worrying?' asked Mary late on Tuesday.

'Nothing I can't handle,' Beth returned. 'I never realised how much in-house work we've accumulated.' She looked around the double room, where six women of varying ages were concentrating on their word-processing terminals.

'Word-of-mouth advertising,' Mary chuckled. 'And we've a funny one in the corner there. Rona has it.'

'Funny?'

'Yes. It came with a letter asking for complete secrecy. A novel, no less, dictated on to cassette tapes. You wouldn't guess who the author is. He's very popular.'

'Don't tell me,' groaned Beth.

'OK, I won't.'

'That's not what I meant,' Beth snapped. 'It's Frank Cranston, isn't it?'

'So that's the way the cookie crumbles,' Mary said softly, her solemn eyes probing green ones that stared at her.

'Don't make a big thing out of it,' Beth returned —and then had a change of heart. 'I'm sorry, Mary, I didn't mean to snap at you—it's just that—I was so surprised.'

'Yes, I can see you were,' the Italian girl giggled.

'You guessed the name first crack. That tells me something.'

'It surely does. It tells you that I read terrible books. Don't make a molehill out of this mountain, dear.'

'It's the other way around.'

'Oh? What?'

'Telephone call for Miss Murphy,' the voice on the speaker system announced. 'Line two.' It was a good excuse to get out of a conversation that wasn't going at all in the right direction. Beth moved over to her desk and picked up the instrument.

'Miss Murphy here.'

'Murphy, this is Rich Macomber.'

'I—hello, Mr Macomber. What's the trouble? Is the bill too high?'

'Not at all,' he laughed. 'In fact it's quite small for the amount of work accomplished. No, I called to thank you again for your efforts on our behalf over the last two weeks. I find it hard to adjust to seeing Grace at the desk where you ought to be.'

'I—thank you—I think,' she returned, blushing. 'I trust your regular secretary is in good health?'

'I'm not too sure about that,' he mused. 'Oh, she's physically healthy. Like myself, a few scratches and bruises. But I'm not sure she doesn't need more time off. She can't seem to get the computer system working again. We're at a sort of stand-off down here.'

'That's too bad, Mr Macomber.'

'Rich,' he insisted. 'You don't work for me any more. I insist, Rich.'

'Er—yes, Rich. I'm sorry your computer is on the blink. I suppose things are a little confused?'

'Like a madhouse. People are running up and down the halls wringing their hands. Maggie is threatening to quit. I don't quite know what to do.'

'Why don't you telephone the software company?' Beth suggested. 'I think it was the Halmen Software Company, in Los Angeles.'

'A good idea,' he agreed. 'Why didn't I think of that? You're good for us, Murphy. Are you sure you wouldn't want to give up that company of yours and come to work here permanently?'

'I don't think so,' she said, brought back to earth suddenly. 'My father used to say I was a good thing, in small doses. If you were to know me better, you might regret it.'

'I doubt that very much,' he returned seriously. 'But thank you, Beth, very much. Goodbye.'

Beth put down the instrument carefully, unwilling to risk dropping it from her shaking fingers. The time-bomb she had just activated was ticking away somewhere, marking the hours until it would explode in his face, and Beth Murphy was frightened by what she had done.

The afternoon was warm, and a contented quiet lay across South Boston as she made her way to the baseball field. 'Two more games to go, kids,' she announced to all her little players. 'And already we've won more games than we did all last year! Everybody here?'

She looked around, counting heads, looking for one in particular, and not finding it.

'She's comin'!' her catcher called. Beth turned around toward the street. The big limousine was there, and Althea climbed out, looking strangely incongruous in her battered uniform.

'Your uncle couldn't come?' asked Beth.

'Nope. He's got some terrible trouble where he works,' the little girl chirped. 'They didn't have trouble like this when you was runnin' the place, Miss Beth. Where do I play today?'

Beth tried to hide the satisfied smile, as she puzzled

over her line-up card. 'We're playing two tough teams this week,' she told the children. 'Tonight we play the fourth-place team, Friday we play the leaders. So—let's see—Frankie will start as pitcher. Michael, you warm up and be ready in case Frank needs relief. Althea will pitch Friday.' She pencilled in all the names, showed them to the players, and dispatched the listing to the officials. 'Now get out there and win me another game!' she yelled. With a large number of happy grins on their faces they charged out into the field, and did just that.

Stacy came home on Wednesday, not as early as expected, but early enough. The girl wore what looked to be a perpetual frown on her doll-like face. 'You're not feeling well?' asked Beth as she made lunch.

'Not that again,' the girl groaned. 'I feel fine. Only—I'm a little mixed-up. Is everything settled about Roddy?'

'Not quite everything,' her aunt said, 'but it's all well in hand. As a guess, I would suppose he can hold out until Friday. So maybe the wedding will be on Monday. How does that suit you?'

'I—I guess that would be fine. It's a big step, isn't it, Aunt Beth. How come you never got married?'

'If I tell, would you keep it a secret?'

'Cross my heart.'

'Did you know there are two women for every available man in the United States?'

'No. Is that true? Is that why you haven't married?'

'It's true,' Beth sighed, 'and I haven't married because nobody ever asked me.'

'But you're so pretty, Aunt Beth.'

'Thank you, love, for those kind words. Unfortunately, when fishing in the matrimonial sea, you need not only the right bait, but a sure knowledge of where the fish are swimming. Right?'

'I—suppose so. I guess I don't know all that much about men. I just thought you only had to be pretty.'

'Hey, don't be so glum! I'm not about to go jump off the Hancock building, you know. There are worse things than being a spinster. And I have all of you children to mother. Eat your steak. I got it especially for you.'

The smile she earned was reward enough for all her pains and worries. By bedtime, after calling her father and mother, Stacy had made Beth feel like a million dollars. And so to bed, early.

It was not until Friday, another dull rainy day in Beantown, that the show began. He called personally, at about eleven o'clock. She took the phone in hand with some trepidation.

'Murphy,' he said gruffly, 'I'm in a great deal of trouble.'

'Oh, how can that be?'

'The computer is still shut down, my editors are running around like chickens with their heads cut off—and that damn software company which sold us the whole affair has burned down. They claim they might be able to reconstruct their records in thirty days—starting the day after their strike ends.'

'Why, that's terrible, Mr Macomber.'

'And we're coming up on some advertising deadlines that would make your head spin. So, I wondered, Murphy——'

'Yes?'

'If you would come over here and take a look at the whole mess? We would pay well, of course.'

'Through the nose, so to speak?'

'Anything.'

Beth let him hang for a moment. She had practised this whole scene in her mind for days, and knew just what had to be said and done. Now, at the launch

point, nervousness attacked. There was only one
way to hold on—think of poor little Stacy, moving
inexorably towards that date which she could not
avoid. Poor little Stacy. 'I'll be over by one o' clock,'
she told him, and hung up gently.

There was a little tight smile on her face as she
walked upstairs. Stacy was giving dusting a bad
name, and welcomed the chance to abandon the
whole project. 'It's too early for lunch, Aunt Beth.'

'I know, dear. I'm too nervous to eat. I have to
make a special trip. This afternoon I want you to
take my credit card and go up to Filene's. Buy
yourself a nice sensible little dress. Something to get
married in.'

'Oh?' Not the most enthusiastic approach to a
wedding announcement Beth had ever heard. Oh?

'Are you having second thoughts, love?'

'I—no. If Roddy wants me, I'll—stick to it.'

'Tell me now, Stacy, or——'

'For ever hold my peace? I'm ready, Aunt Beth.'

Beth sat on the edge of her own bed for a few
minutes, calming her nerves. What to wear to a
confrontation? Armour plate, or a plain dark suit?
The suit won, hands down. A tailored chocolate
jacket and skirt, and a beige blouse beneath it.
Utmost dignity, right! And her hair up on the top
of her head, leaving her classic silhouette exposed.
Glasses. She only needed them for reading, but they
added a delicate touch of firmness. Dark tights,
brown shoes—with the highest heels she owned. It's
no use trying to stand up to a man when he towers
over you for ever and ever.

One cab for both of them, to drop Stacy off, and
then wind back to the Financial District, and leave
Beth at the building near Liberty Square.

'Good to see you again, Miss Murphy,' Sam the
doorman called as he swung the heavy lobby doors

open for her. 'It's been mighty strange here since you've been gone.'

'Is that so, Sam? Well, I'm only here for a short visit. How's your wife?'

'Doing well, miss. Strange, you should be the only one in the building to ask. I brought her home from the hospital last week, and the daughter is there to help take care of her. It's a shame about these new medical restrictions. Can you imagine, she has pneumonia, so she can only stay in hospital for ten days. Nothing to do with how well she is, or anything. It's just a Federal regulation!'

'It does seem strange, Sam. Give her my regards.'

Beth went into the empty lobby, wondering if she should take time for a quick cup of coffee in the cafeteria. Her stomach counselled otherwise. It growled under the nervous strain. She stopped in front of the elevator and took three or four deep breaths.

There was never a thought for the stairs. She stepped into the little box. If it broke down—left her between floors somehow—that would be a sign from God to stop what she was doing! She leaned back against the wall, and crossed the middle fingers on each hand. Something looked different. The empty little machine had been redecorated. The walls were now a bright yellow, and a thick-piled rug covered the formerly bare floor. 'Window dressing,' she muttered to herself, and resolutely pushed the button.

God was making no effort to intervene at Liberty Square that day. The elevator shook and wheezed and groaned, but managed to stagger up to the fourth floor without a major catastrophe. When its doors opened, Beth hung back, almost wishing for something to happen. Something did.

Maggie Berman popped out of her office next to the elevator, started down the hall, then recognised

her. 'Beth Murphy! Well, thank God you've come!
Hurry!'

'Hurry?' Beth was *being* hurried. The Editor-in-
Chief had seized her arm and was dragging her
along the hall towards the executive suite. 'It isn't
that we've forgotten how to process books by hand,'
Maggie chattered, 'but everything is in that damn
computer, and we can't get a single read-out to work
on. Forty-six manuscripts, all eaten up by the
machine!'

'You don't have spare copies?'

'Sure we do. All on disks. All tied up in the works!
You've got to do something, Beth. Blow the roof
off, or something.' Maggie was pushing her into the
office at the end of the hall by now, and abandoning
her.

And that's exactly what I've come for, Beth told
herself, building up her courage. To blow the roof
off! They'll hear the explosion all the way to Govern-
ment Center. I wonder if I'll survive? She shuddered,
and walked very slowly across the outer office. The
door to the inner office opened.

'No, I don't mean it as any criticism of you,
Grace. Dear God, don't cry at me! I know you're
just out of the hospital, and——' He seemed to
falter, but the tiny blonde girl tucked under his left
arm was enjoying her ill health. Beyond his eye level,
her baby blues were sparkling. Until she saw Beth.
The sparkle disappeared, and the tears overflowed.
Rich Macomber looked up.

'Murphy. Thank God you've come!' It was heart-
felt enthusiasm. Which threw Beth off-centre, and
accelerated the tears of the little blonde bombshell.
'Now, Grace. You sit right here. I've called for the
nurse. She's going to come up, and then will arrange
to send you home.' Another wail, more tears. 'There,
there now,' he mumbled, helping the girl into a

chair. 'I don't know what to do,' he muttered in Beth's direction.

'Me neither,' said Beth. There was something about this fountain of tears that seemed too unreal. Either the girl was a splendid actress—or—or was horribly humiliated. Either way, it's no skin off my nose, Beth told herself fiercely. I didn't come all this way, do all these terrible things, to end up acting friendly in the face of the enemy. That's what he is. The enemy. Keep saying that, over and over!

The nurse appeared at the door. Beth stood out of the line of fire, repeating her little litany over and over again. When the two of them, Grace and the nurse, disappeared down the hall, Macomber wiped his forehead. 'I can't stand weepy women,' he sighed. And then, more cheerfully, 'But I'm glad you came. If anyone can straighten out this mess, you can.'

'How right you are,' she said coldly. She brushed by him, dropped into the secretarial chair, and tested the computer terminal. Everything was as she had programmed it. No matter what passwords were offered, the computer continued to flash back 'Access denied'. Now, make it look good, she told herself. She turned off the terminal, moving slowly, and stood up.

'I know what the trouble is, Mr Macomber,' she said flatly. 'I think we'd better go into your office to discuss it.'

'Is it that bad?' A frown ran across his face. 'But hell, you can do anything, Murphy.'

'You've never said a truer word,' she said brazenly. He started for his inner office. Beth turned on the automatic answering machines, locked the outer door behind her, and followed him in. She closed the inner door softly, and locked it, too. He was at his desk, watching. Those deep, dark eyes of his were hooded, suspicious. He seemed to test the wind, as a nervous wild animal might when he suspects a hunter.

Beth came slowly across the office, keeping the growing excitement off her face. Her unaccustomed heels wobbled in the thick rug, making her progression a swaying strut. He watched her closely as she chose a chair and sank into it.

Macomber went around his desk and settled in his own chair. One of his hands tapped on the top of his desk. He touched a letter, straightening it out, and then laid a pencil on top of it at a precise angle. 'I have the vague idea that you're going to tell me something that I'm not going to like,' he sighed.

Take one good look, Beth told herself. He's a fine man—the sort of person Mother would have liked to meet. But Stacy needs him. And when I've finished here today he would probably sooner spit on me than talk. If I'm lucky he might only beat me up. I could have loved a man like him. I really could. But there's no turning back.

'I know what's wrong with your computer, Mr Macomber,' she said. It was hard to keep her voice level. It tended to quiver and shoot up-scale. A squeak would just not do. She *had* to have dignity.

He waited, tapping at the corner of his desk with one hand, the other out of sight below the level of the desk-top.

'Your computer has been sabotaged.'

Not a muscle moved in his face. He looked like an Egyptian Pharaoh, carved in stone. She watched for some question, some doubt, some difference. There was nothing to be seen. Her fingers twisted in her lap. It was proving harder and harder to do, this task she had set for herself—for little Stacy.

'You heard me?'

He nodded.

She swallowed hard, and began again, tentatively.

'Somebody has changed all the passwords in every department and on every account. The machine is locked against any penetration. The only people who could unlock it would be the programmers at Halmen Software, and——'

'They're unable to help,' he said firmly. 'The plant has burned down, and there's a strike on. You said "and"?'

'I know they're out of business,' she whispered. 'And that means I'm the only one who can unlock the computer.'

He made a tent out of his fingers, holding them up under his chin, and then putting them down out of sight again. 'I see, Murphy. The computer has been sabotaged, and you're the only one who can make it right. It follows, then, that you're the one who sabotaged it in the first place.'

'I—yes.'

'So that only leaves us one question. Why?'

'This isn't easy for me,' she stammered. 'I——'

'I don't intend to make it easy for you,' he snapped. His voice was like a whiplash, slashing at her shoulders. She flinched. 'Why, Murphy?'

'I—I have a niece,' she managed to get out. 'Anastasia Murphy. About five foot two—a lovely *young* blonde girl.' She emphasised the word young. The saying gave her courage. Poor Stacy, and here was the rapist, sitting right in front of her.

'And I'm supposed to know this Anastasia? God, what a name for a little Irish girl!'

'Yes, you know her!' snarled Beth. 'You know her very well, you damn—monster! She was that cute little student that you played around with at Marymont College! Now do you remember?'

'You don't have to scream, Murphy. Marymont College? The girls' college next door to Cornell University, right?'

'You can't fool me, Mr Macomber. You know darn well who she is, and where Marymont is.'

'My! My memory must be slipping.'

'I can well imagine that it might, Roddy Macomber.' She could swear that a flash of startled interest had just moved across his face, but it was so quick—and he reverted back to solemnity so fast, that she just wasn't sure. In fact, there was a gleam in his eye, one that hadn't been there before. He leaned forward in his chair, the springs squeaking as his considerable weight changed. 'Tell me more,' he said softly.

The words seemed to drift across the room at her. drawing her to him. She shook herself, and sat up straight, both feet flat on the floor.

'You had your fun, Mr Macomber,' she snapped. 'And now——'

'Oh God, not that old cliché—and now it's time to pay the piper.' He mimicked her accent, her tone. He's laughing at me! she screamed at herself.

'Yes. Exactly. Now it's time to pay the piper. Stacy is pregnant!' And try *that* on for size, playboy, she thought. He seemed to be thinking it over. He leaned back in his chair, those hooded eyes telling her nothing. But he took the pencil with him, twirling it between his fingers.

'So what you're telling me, Murphy, is that some man has gotten to your sweet little niece, and I'm nominated as the leading candidate. Not so?'

'Exactly.'

'You know it would be almost impossible to prove such a charge?'

'I know it, Mr Macomber. But I know it's true, Stacy knows it's true, and you know it's true! That's why I hijacked your computer!'

'Ah! So that's what's going on, is it? You're holding my computer up for ransom. Why, I do believe that's blackmail, Murphy.'

'Yes it is,' she admitted. 'Blackmail. And I've got all the cards in my hand! Well?'

'Not that I'm admitting any such thing, Murphy, but what do you see as coming next? It's support money, damages, that sort of thing?'

'It's got nothing to do with money,' she snapped. 'The child is not going to be born a——' She hesitated at the word. He supplied it.

'Bastard, you mean. Isn't that the old-fashioned word for it?'

'I—I was going to say—illegitimate,' she stuttered. 'We Murphys don't believe in that sort of thing.'

'Come on now, Murphy,' he chuckled. 'There isn't a family in the world that hasn't had to deal with bastardy once or twice over the years. So it's not money—what is it you want?'

'I should think it's plain enough!' she yelled at him. 'I demand that you marry my niece!'

He grinned at her. A wolfish grin—the sort of thing that any well brought up girl should have recognised—and run from. But Beth Murphy was too deep in her Crusader's role to notice.

'I expect that you'll do the right thing and marry the girl,' she repeated stubbornly. His finger went back to the desk top. Tap, tap, tap.

'You say all this happened in up-state New York?'

'You know darn well it did. You were there. You did it. Sweet talk and innocence. Damn all you playboys! You'll not get away with it this time, Mr Macomber.'

'No, I can see I won't,' he said, so smoothly that if her nose were in tune she would have smelled a rat. Instead, she accepted it on its face value, and relaxed, falling against the back of her chair as if she had just run in the Boston Marathon. All her bones ached, her stomach was upset, but she could feel victory in her grasp.

'So just how will we go about this—er—marriage?' he asked.

'Something in front of a Justice of the Peace.' She shuddered to think of it. Any girl would want a big church wedding. It was the custom in Irish families; it was something that life owed her. And poor Stacy. But it was better than—what he said.

'I suppose I could find something,' he went on. 'I know a judge in the Superior Court who would be willing, I'm sure. Would that be satisfactory?'

The sound of his voice was getting to her now. It was just a little *too* oily. You're dealing with a slippery customer, she warned herself. Be careful. This—monster—has probably deflowered dozens of girls like Stacy.

'It would have to be some judge I could check up on,' she said carefully. 'And in his court.'

'Ah! Most commendable,' he laughed. 'Don't let the worm wiggle out from under with a fake judge, huh? You read too many of our Regency Romances, Murphy. I suppose you'd want something down in writing, too?'

'You're darn well right,' she retorted. It was something she hadn't thought of before, but it was certainly a good idea. Just because it came from him shouldn't make it a poor thought!

She came up out of her chair, all five foot eight inches of her, including two-inch heels. He grinned as she walked over to the desk. He opened a drawer and pulled out a pad of paper. 'Something simple, I suppose?'

'Yes,' she agreed hoarsely. 'Something simple that a stupid secretary could understand!'

'OK, how about this?' He wrote quickly as he spoke. 'It is agreed by the undersigned, that Mr

Macomber will marry—what did you say her name was?'

'Anastasia!'

'Imagine that. Anastasia Murphy. I can't spell that. Why don't I just make it Miss Murphy?'

'That—sounds all right,' she said hesitantly. 'Yes.'

He continued to write, finishing with a flourish. 'It is agreed between the undersigned that Mr Macomber will marry Miss Murphy on Monday, June 8, 198-n the Suffolk County Court House at eleven o' clock in the morning.' He scribbled his signature at the bottom of the paper and turned it around to face her. 'Of course, you recognise there might be some change in time. I'll have to check with Judge Morrissey for that.'

Now that victory was within her grasp, Beth hesitated. It wasn't just suspicion. It was rather that facing such a final act and putting it on paper only re-emphasised how far out of her *own* life she would have to put them. She was not aware of the mute appeal on her face as she took his pen and signed her name just below his. He took the paper from her, and lifted the pen from her nerveless fingers.

'I forgot to date it,' he said, as he made that correction at the top of the paper.

She backed up to her chair, and fell into it, her mind working, looking for loopholes. 'How about the licence?' she blurted out.

'I forgot that,' he admitted. 'Well, let's see. I can get that today. There's a three-day waiting period. Working days, that is. That makes it—Wednesday before we can do it. Shall I make that change?'

She nodded at him, helpless to bring out the words. He crossed out the word Monday on the paper and substituted Wednesday. 'Now you have to initial that change,' he ordered. She came back to the desk and did so, moving like a zombie.

'Now then,' he said. 'Would you mind unlocking my computer?'

'Oh, no, you don't,' she said firmly. 'I wasn't born yesterday.'

'Certainly not,' he laughed. 'But I'm not sure about the day before that!'

'*What* do you mean?'

'Nothing,' he sighed, shaking his head. 'About my computer?'

'Oh, I'll unlock it,' she stammered. 'Right after the wedding. When you take Stacy off I'll come by and—and do it.'

'And in the meantime my staff is to sit on its hands and wait around?'

'Be big-hearted,' she sighed. 'It's your wedding. Give them a couple of days off. You can afford it.'

'Yes, I suppose I can,' he returned. 'It will be something to celebrate, won't it? I don't suppose you would want to come to a reception after the affair?'

'I don't suppose I would,' she said. 'Not that you shouldn't have one. Do, by all means. It would make a nice touch. I feel very badly for Stacy—but a girl who's pregnant can't afford to wait for too many nice touches.'

'No, I don't suppose she can,' he said, and the words almost had a touch of kindness to them. That's all it would need, Beth screamed at herself. A touch of kindness and I'll come apart at the seams. There'll be so many tears running down Broad Street they'll think it's a repetition of the Great Molasses Flood. Stand tall, girl!

'Well,' he mused, 'the wedding, the agreement, the licence, the judge, the place, the time. Is there anything we could have left out?'

'If there is I'll call you,' she said. 'I—I'll come to

the wedding with Stacy—to stand up for her, you know.'

'That's a quaint thought. I'll get my nephew to do the same. He'll be in town that day.'

'And Althea?'

'For the wedding? I don't think so.'

'I—suppose she won't be coming to our last games?'

'Whatever gave you that idea? Of course she'll be coming. She'll have my head if I get her dropped off the team.'

'Well, that's all right then.' A couple of sniffs were not enough to hold back the tears. Beth fumbled in her bag for the little lace scrap she carried around for emergencies, and dabbed at her eyes.

'Will you look at that,' Macomber commented coolly. 'Two women in a row, running to tears in my office.'

'I'm sure it's not a record,' she muttered at him. 'With your track record I suppose there are dozens of women who've cried over you.'

'Maybe even thousands,' he said. 'Is that what you're doing—crying over me, Murphy?'

'No, of course not,' she snapped. 'Why would I do a thing like that? I'm crying over Stacy. Poor kid. Her life's barely begun, and she's—trapped into this horrible mess!'

'We could always call it off,' he suggested.

'Never!' Her head came up and she glared at him. 'Never. It's the only thing to do. And if you try anything fancy, Mr Macomber, your company is going to be out of business until the Halmen Company rebuilds, or hell freezes over——'

'Which ever comes first,' he laughed. 'Well, it's been a fun afternoon, Murphy. One that will stick in my mind for a long time to come. I can safely say I've never had an afternoon like this in all my life. So there's only one more thing to do.'

He came up out of his chair and stalked around the desk, looking for all the world like a hunting animal in the jungle. Alarmed, Beth struggled to her feet. 'What else?' she whispered.

'Why, it's a poor bargain if we don't seal it with a kiss,' he said. For some reason her words and her mouth would not match. She managed a stutter or two before his arms were around her, pulling her in close against his chest. And by that time, words were beyond her capacity.

His soft, sweet lips came down on hers, sealing them, as well as the bargain, with an impulse that throbbed through her body like a new Paul Revere, riding through Middlesex County crying 'The British are coming!' For a moment she drew back, thinking of Stacy. But deep within her a voice yelled, 'Stacy will have him for the rest of her life. Surely you can have a minute?'

She stopped fighting. He had drawn off for that second when she stiffened, thinking. When she relaxed he returned to the work, shutting her off from the world with his inciting lips, his roaming hands, and the pressure of his hips against hers. She lost herself in the glory of it, savouring every second, until she was no longer passive in his arms, but had become a participant.

His hands came to rest just below the inward swell of her waist, and pulled her lower body forward into more intimate contact. Her own hands fluttered at his neck, his shoulders, and finally slipped inside his jacket, and around his back. Not all the way around; her reach was too small for that. And when he broke contact with his lips she huddled closer, resting her head on his chest, listening to nothing in the world but his heartbeat.

It carried a message, and she read it. 'You've

given up more than the world,' it said, over and over again. She stood it for as long as she could, but finally it brought the tears back. Her long, slender fingers pushed against him, and he let her go. She took two steps backwards, looked up at his stone face, and whimpered.

'Murphy?' he asked.

She whirled away farther, stabbed at her clouded eyes, and ran. The locked door held her up for a moment. Her fingers were shaking too much to turn the key. He came up behind her, silent, and did it for her. When the door gave, she moaned once, and ran again. Not the elevator. The stairs. Not because of doubt, but because of fear. Ghosts were trailing her as she darted down the interminable flights. When she burst out into the lobby, barely able to see, Sam came over and caught her arm.

'Mr Macomber called down,' he said. 'You're to take the limousine to get home.' He led her through the double doors and out to the kerb, where the car waited. Inside, she broke down again, sobbing her heart out. The chauffeur needed no directions. He took her straight home.

Stacy was waiting for her when she arrived. The girl was modelling a beautiful white silk dress, a simple understated design, that clung to her in all the right places, and enhanced her youthful innocence. Beth stabbed at her eyes, swallowed her tears, and put all regrets behind her.

'It's settled, love,' she told her niece. 'Next Wednesday, at eleven o' clock in the morning.'

'Roddy said he would?'

'Yes,' Beth sighed, and wandered off to her room. Inside, lying sprawled out on the bed, she ran her mental tape over and over again, trying to find loopholes, errors, ways of escape. And found none.

CHAPTER NINE

STACY'S wedding day dawned poorly. A deadly hush lay over the city, as an inversion was locked in place by a Bermuda high. Not a speck of breeze blew. The air was thick enough to eat, and Health Commission warnings were being broadcast over every radio station. Beth watched it all from the shadows of her front porch. At six in the morning, unable to sleep, worn from her tossing and turning, she got up, slipped into a light robe, and walked out to catch the sunrise. Blood red, it was. 'Red skies at dawning, sailor take warning,' she muttered as she sipped at her coffee mug. It was going to take something stronger than black coffee to keep up her courage this day.

Two pigeons, nesting under the eaves above her head, took that moment to fly. The sudden noise startled Beth, confirming her own diagnosis. There *had* to be something to take her mind off the future. MAC. She shook her head in disgust. Why would a normal woman of twenty-seven find comfort keying a computer?

Because you don't have to think, her brain screamed at her. You can key-punch with the best of them with not a single thought in your narrow brain! It was a potent argument. She went back to her bedroom, slipped into shorts and a halterneck top, and went downstairs.

By the time Stacy was up, near to nine o'clock, Beth was back upstairs. They both were nervous. Breakfast was coffee and toast. The eggs went into the bin, and both went off to dress.

Although there was not a cloud in the sky, the world was almost opaque, as the inversion trapped odours and pollutants under its tent. But, once inside the court-house, things were different. An indifferent bailiff guided them through the maze to Judge Morrissey's office, hidden away behind his court-room. Beth, leading the way, stopped short and caught her breath. The Judge's office was not palatial, but neither was it spartan. Thick brown rugs covered the floor. A huge desk was the centrepiece. Behind it, all the walls were lined with law books. The Judge himself, a thin wiry man, half bald, was standing behind his desk, still in judicial robes, with a big smile, balancing his glasses precariously on the end of his nose.

In front of the desk Richard Macomber waited, dressed quietly in a dark blue suit, white shirt, and neutral tie. Beside him a younger man, dressed the same, was leaning against the desk. The best man, Beth told herself. A relative, from the looks of him. He could be Richard, fifteen years earlier. The same chin, the same hairline, the same eyes—but not the same self-assurance. No indeed!

Beth offered them a wintry smile. Richard responded with that wolf-grin of his, and took a step forward. At that moment Stacy came across the threshold, caught the tableau in one quick look, threw her little bouquet to the wind, and went racing across the room. 'Oh, Roddy,' she half screamed, 'I never really thought it would happen!' And she threw herself at the wrong man!

The younger man paled, tried to evade her grasp, and then blushed. Beth, thunderstruck, was frozen in place—until she felt a shake of her arm, and looked down at Richard's hand rattling her. 'Wrong guess, Murphy?' he asked softly. There was an unholy gleam in his eyes. He's really enjoying this, Beth thought, trembling.

'I think—I wish I could faint,' she muttered. 'You—you knew it all the time, damn you!'

'Why, of course I did.' He lifted her hand to kiss the palm. 'You've been playing in the wrong league, Murphy. His name is Rodman. We call him Roddy.'

'You're darn well right I've been in the wrong league,' she snapped, moving across the room to stand behind her niece. 'And I have a few things to call him myself!'

'Marry you?' Roddy was doing his best to back away from his prospective bride, but with the desk behind him and the girl in front, there was nowhere to go. 'I—I don't want to marry you, Stacy. You're a good kid, but—I'm not ready for——'

'Roddy Macomber, what are you saying? Aunt Beth said you were going to marry me!'

'Well, your Aunt Beth can go soak her head,' Roddy snarled. 'You're not going to trap *me* into something like that!'

'You mean, you don't love me, Roddy?'

'God, what do I have to do, spell it out for you?'

'There's no need for you to talk to my niece like that, young man,' Beth interjected. 'I've made a slight mistake, perhaps, but there's no way you can evade your responsibilities.'

'I don't know what you're talking about, ma'am.'

'Do explain it to him.' Rich Macomber was close behind her, talking almost into her ear. 'Explain to the lad.'

'I will,' Beth snapped. She moved her foot back and stamped with her heel, but he had moved his foot out of the way, and laughed.

'If you're Roddy Macomber,' Beth continued, 'You've done my niece wrong, and——'

'Good work,' came the whisper in her ear. 'Right out of a melodrama!'

'Shut up!' she threw in the general direction of her right shoulder, and then, at the boy in front of her, 'Did you expect you could make my niece pregnant and then sit back and not pay for it? Not a chance. There's going to be a wedding here, believe me!'

'That's telling him,' the voice in her ear approved. 'And you're so right.'

'Pregnant? Who's pregnant?' Stacy dropped her stranglehold on Roddy's arm and turned to her aunt. 'Who's pregnant?'

'Why, you are, dear. And he's going to marry you.'

'I am? I am *not!* Where did you get that crazy idea?'

'But—but——' The world seemed to be going in circles. Beth could see the desk as it swept around her at speed, the lights overhead as they flickered and wavered, the soft rug, as it reached up and enfolded her. At which point Beth Murphy did something she had never done before in all her life.

It must have been some minutes later when things drifted back into focus. Beth was pressed up hard against something strong and warm. There was an arm under her knees, another at her back.

'Would you believe it?' the disbelieving voice of Rich Macomber rumbled at her ear. 'She actually *did* faint!'

'I—I did no such thing,' she managed weakly. 'I never faint. I——'

'Shut up,' Richard told her, very gently.

'So I would suppose there's no need for me—there'll be no wedding?' Judge Morrissey was speaking cautiously, trying to make some sense out of it all.

'Not so, Your Honour. If we might have a few
minutes?'

'Take all the time you want,' the Judge responded.
'I'm free until two o'clock. Use my clerk's office,
next door.'

Beth closed her eyes, and found herself wafted out
of the room in total comfort, and set down in a big
upholstered chair.

'All right, Murphy. You can open your eyes now.
There's no use faking it any longer.'

'Go away,' she stuttered angrily. 'I don't want to
see you or talk to you—or anything.'

'We'll see about the *anything* part,' he said. 'Now,
you two babes in the woods. Just what the hell has
been going on? Do I understand, Anastasia, that
you're not pregnant?'

'Of course not,' the girl snapped. 'I may be young,
but I'm not *that* stupid. You can't get pregnant *that*
way.'

'I wouldn't do a thing like that,' his nephew
whined. 'Good God, I hardly knew the girl!'

'But—but Stacy, when you came to me, you told
me you were in *terrible trouble*. And there was a
man involved. I know it's hard to say the real words,
so I——'

'Well, you thought wrong, Aunt Beth.' The girl
was angry, the boy was angry, the man was laughing,
and I'm in a lot of trouble, Beth told herself.

'So what—what was the problem?' she asked
faintly.

'I'll tell you something, I don't intend to be forced
into marriage just because I——'

'Shut up, Roddy,' his uncle commanded in a very
soft voice. The young man gulped and went silent.
'Stacy, what is this terrible trouble you're in?'

'I—I was suspended from school,' she admitted,
her voice hardly audible.

'You were suspended from school? Why?'

'I—Roddy?'

All eyes shifted to the boy. He squirmed under the examination. 'It was no big thing,' he muttered. 'Stacy was a nice kid, and I wanted to help her, that's all.'

'That's all what?'

'Well, she was about to flunk out in Freshman biology. I'm majoring in biology, so I loaned her one of my old Senior term papers.'

'Ah!' Two exclamations, one triumphant, the other mortified.

'And what happened?'

'Well, I thought she would copy out a few paragraphs. Would you believe how stupid that girl is——'

'Don't call my niece stupid!'

'Hush, Murphy.' That soft command, again.

'Well, I happen to think it's stupid. She submitted the whole paper. Did nothing but take my name off the thing and put hers on. I can't imagine what she was thinking of. I won Senior biology honours with that paper, and she submits it as a Freshman term paper. Dumb!' Roddy shook his wise twenty-four year old head in disgust.

'And so then what happened?' Rich Macomber again, with a broad smile on his face. I'd like to punch him in the mouth, Beth thought. He must have been reading her mind, for he moved a pace or two away from her chair.

'Well, you know how colleges are. Stacy's instructor met mine one night and was boasting about her prize student—and it all came out! Boy, did the discipline committee come down on me!'

Silence ruled the roost, until Beth stirred out of her shock and propelled herself over to her niece. 'There now, love,' she comforted, holding the girl in her arms. 'I'm sorry. I really am. I don't suppose you'd want to marry Roddy, after all?'

The girl lifted her little doll face. There were tears running down her cheeks. 'I wouldn't marry that jerk if he were the last man in the world!' she retorted. 'Men are nothing but large pains in the—the neck. And I didn't need any more help, either. My father warned me about you, too. All those crazy ideas you have. Boy, this is wild enough for me. I'm going to be a nun!'

An inexplicable rage filled her aunt. 'I don't know about being a nun,' Beth said stiffly, 'I'll tell you what you're *going* to be,' she returned. 'You're going to be on the next flight back to California, if I have to hock my watch to pay for the ticket.'

'What a lovely idea,' Richard added sarcastically. 'I tell you what, I'll share the cost of the ticket. And as for you, Roddy——'

'I—I know, Uncle Rich.'

'Do you really? I think you've had enough of a scare for one day. You can spend the rest of the week in Boston with your grandmother, and then it's back to school for you—and you can borrow my Jaguar for the trip.'

'Oh, wow!'

'Yes. Oh, wow! Now the pair of you get out of here. Wait for us out in the Judge's office, and tell him we'll only be a minute.'

The two young people walked out of the room, each acting as if the other didn't exist. Beth returned to her chair and slumped into it, exhausted. Richard stood watching her for a minute, then pulled up another chair and confronted her, face to face.

'Now, we have things to talk about,' he began.

'I—can't imagine what,' she sighed. 'I admit it was a terrible mess. I suppose I should go and apologise to the Judge?'

'That won't be necessary. There's still going to be a wedding.' She came up straight in her chair. There was that look about him, the hunting look.

'I don't know what you mean,' she said firmly. 'I'm sorry for the—the inconvenience I've caused, but——'

'Inconvenience!' he roared. 'Is that what you call it? One hundred and forty people on my payroll, sitting around doing nothing because of your fool scheme. You call that nothing?'

'You don't have to yell at me,' she said. 'It was—perhaps—a little extreme, but desperate causes require desperate solutions.' She stirred uneasily in her chair. His glare had not receded one whit, and the silence was making her jittery.

'Now, about our wedding.'

'Our wedding? Why in the world would you want to marry me?'

'Don't you ever look in a mirror, woman? Good lord, why would anyone in his right mind not want to marry you?'

'I told you I don't plan to do any such a thing!' She struggled up out of her chair, clutching her bag desperately to her breast. 'I—I don't even *like* you, Mr Macomber.'

'Liking has nothing to do with it,' he rasped. 'I need a wife. You're suitable. Very suitable. And you owe me. So we'll get married.'

'Damn you.' She struggled against the tears. 'I might be suitable—but you're not. You have a terrible reputation, and I can't believe that you just would marry some woman because she's—suitable!'

'Ah, but we have an agreement, you and I.'

'What are you talking about? What agreement?'

His grin had returned, that face-filling wolfish look. He took a paper out from his inner jacket pocket, unfolded it, and laid it out on the table.

'Right there, in black and white. "It is agreed that Mr Macomber and Miss Murphy will marry . . . " and so forth. Your signature at the bottom?'

'Of course it's my signature, but—but that has nothing to do with *you* and *me* getting married. That's just——'

'Signed and sealed, Murphy. A valid contract.'

'It is *not!*' she shouted at him. 'Not in Massachusetts, at least. Breach of promise suits specifying marriage have been outlawed in this state for over thirty years. So there, Mr Macomber.'

'A lawyer as well!' She flinched at the tone. It sounded like the rattling of chains and manacles, ghosts marching over her grave.

'Anybody knows that,' she whispered, deserted by all her courage. 'It's not legal.'

'Perhaps not,' he said softly. Her head snapped up. She had come to know at least this about him—he was most dangerous when he was talking softly. His hand was in his jacket pocket. He pulled it out slowly. Beth watched, hardly able to breathe. He set the little plastic box out on the desk. 'A portable tape recorder, Miss Murphy. You've seen them? I couldn't do without one in my business. Capable of recording everything said anywhere in the room. Did you know that?'

'No, I didn't,' she snapped. 'So what?'

'So listen, Murphy.' His fingers slid along the top of the tape recorder. A button clicked, and the hiss of tape running could be heard loud and clear. And then a voice. Her voice. And then his. 'But that's blackmail,' he was saying. And she was agreeing, eager to finish her explanation.

'What—what was that?' she gasped.

'In my office last week,' he purred. 'You remember. When you came in and blackmailed me into marrying your niece?'

'I—what—does that have to do with us?'

'Knees shaky, Murphy? Why don't you sit down? And then I'll tell you.'

She fell back into her chair, both hands nervously twisting against each other in her lap, her forgotten handbag on the floor.

'Now, I'll go slowly so you can follow me. You are a blackmailer. That's a felony crime in this state. Five to ten years in jail, I believe. Now, you have two choices. Either you put a big smile on your face and we go out and have Judge Morrissey marry us——'

'Or?'

'Or I call the police and press blackmail charges against you.'

'You can't force me to marry you,' she said. 'You don't have a marriage licence for us.'

'Is that a fact?' That soft voice again, with the smile behind it. 'Will you just look, Murphy? I have a marriage licence. For Mr Macomber and Miss Murphy, with the first names blank. How about that! Now, all I have to do is to write in my name—Richard—right   there,   and   your name—Elizabeth—right there. You know, it's lucky you and your niece have the same number of letters in your name. There's just enough space for Anastasia or Elizabeth. Wasn't that clever planning? You even had a physical exam in time for the blood test!'

'You—you couldn't have planned this all that long ago. You just couldn't!'

'Isn't that strange?' There was a tiny smile on his face. 'Maybe it was just—fortuitous? That's a word I always wanted to use, and never knew where to use it! Any more arguments?'

Beth slumped down in the chair, her mind racing. Jail or marriage? Which was worse? Marriage, under different circumstances, might be heaven with this

man. But not under compulsion. Not a dictatorial
'you suit my requirements'.

'I'll marry you,' she said through clenched teeth.
But you'll not get any pleasure out of it, Mr
Macomber. Indeed you will not!

'Ah, how nice. And how enthusiastic,' he retorted.
'You overwhelm me with your desires. Nothing
more to say?'

'Get it over with,' she muttered. 'Stop chattering
like a baboon.'

'Good. I like the idea of a wife who's in a hurry!'
He came around the desk, all smiles, took her arm,
and escorted her out into the Judge's office. Roddy
and Stacy were sitting on opposite sides of the room.
They both jumped up guiltily. The Judge, leaning
back in his big swivel-chair, smiled.

'Stacy, your Aunt Beth and I have decided to get
married. Haven't we, sweetheart?' Richard gave
Beth's arm a shake.

'Yes,' she muttered.

'Oh, how wonderful, Aunt Beth!' Stacy swarmed
all over her, face alight with enthusiasm.

'Yes,' she returned, hugging the girl. 'Wonderful.'
My face will split in pieces if I smile, she warned
herself. She looked over at the Judge. 'Could we do
it now, please?'

They could. With minimum effort they were
married. Rich prodded her twice when she was
required to speak. She managed the words stiffly,
but no one else seemed to notice. It was over before
she knew. Roddy and Stacy signed as witnesses, the
Judge completed the forms, kissed the bride, and
they were out of the door, man and wife.

'Now that wasn't hard, was it?' Richard was still
holding her arm as they stood outside the court-
house, waiting for his limousine to come around.

'No,' Beth managed to say. 'Not hard. Just impossible.' She shook her arm, but could not get free. 'Please,' she begged. He looked down, almost as if he had forgotten. The hand released. She rubbed the spot on her arm, glad that she had worn a dress with sleeves. There would be marks on her skin for days.

'Roddy,' he said, handing his nephew a set of keys, 'the car is over at Liberty Square. You'll have to spend the week at your grandmother's house. And you make sure you're out of Boston by the end of the week. You hear me?'

'I hear.' Roddy took the keys just as the limousine came along. 'I congratulate you, Uncle,' the boy laughed. 'Better you than me!'

'Smart kid,' said Richard as he ushered the two women into the car. 'I was a lot like that when I was young. We'll go home now.'

'I don't think so,' Beth said stubbornly. She leaned forward towards the chauffeur. 'Logan Airport,' she commanded. The driver looked around to Macomber for confirmation, and received a nod.

'But I don't have any of my clothes or things,' Stacy wailed.

'Not to worry,' her aunt told her coldly. 'You'll be home in four hours. I'll call your father to meet you at the airport. I'll mail your things. And Stacy—if you ever think of running to your Aunt Beth again—don't do it!'

'All right, Aunt Beth. I'm really sorry. And I'll tell Mom and Dad all about your wedding. They'll be surprised. Dad said you would never get married. That you were an ideal maiden aunt, and a confirmed spinster.' Beth winced at the enthusiasm, but patted the girl's head in loving fashion.

They were just in time at the airport. Beth was still in a daze. Richard bustled around the terminal at the height of efficiency, found Stacy a seat, bought the ticket, and provided her with an armful of reading matter. They waited until the plane had left on its way to Dallas. During all this time Beth moved like an automaton, following instructions, holding up her cheek to be kissed, and studying the ring on her finger.

It was some sort of sign, that ring. A mark of her total degradation? A brand of his possession? Her mind was just too confused to take it all in. She and Rich were back in the limousine before she came to the surface.

'My brother Fred,' she remembered. 'We have to call Fred. The poor child will be all alone in the Los Angeles airport, and——'

He sighed. 'Stacy and I called him before she left.'

'Oh, that's nice.' Her voice was low, uninterested, flat. She fell back into her stupor again, huddled in the far corner of the capacious back seat. Her eyes saw nothing. Not the clutter of East Boston and the tunnels, nor the strained look in the eyes of her new husband, who studied her silently until the car drew up outside the Harbor Towers.

Mrs Moore, all smiles, met them at the door. 'Did you do it?'

'We did it. She had some doubts, but we did it. Where's Althea?'

'She won't be back until six o'clock. In fact, I thought I would call down and have Frank go after her. Lunch?'

'Beth?'

'Mrs Macomber?'

Beth had hardly moved a muscle. Her face was cold and distant, her mind a million miles away. Rich touched her shoulder. She flinched, and then looked up.

'Lunch?' Mrs Moore repeated.

'No, I'm not hungry,' Beth returned. Every word

seemed to be an effort. Every movement had its pain.

'I think perhaps we've tired her out,' Richard told the housekeeper. 'Why don't you make us something we can warm up and then you can be on your way, Mrs Moore.'

'I'd hate to leave so soon. Mrs Macomber —doesn't look well. I'd just as soon wait until later . . .'

'No, no need for that. I can look after my wife with no trouble at all. And now that I think of it, perhaps you could call my mother and ask her to keep Althea overnight?'

He didn't wait for an answer. His hand went to Beth's arm, guiding her gently across the living-room, down the corridor, and into the master bedroom. He brought her to the centre of the room. She stayed there, deep in her misery, while he did other things. The door to the apartment finally slammed behind the housekeeper, and Rich was back at her side.

'I thought you might prefer us to be alone,' he told her. 'Here, let me help you with that jacket.' She held her arms out like a little child as he slipped the blazer off her shoulders. 'I guess we *have* worn you out. Perhaps you'd better climb into bed and take a nap. In fact, why don't we *both* climb in and take a nap?'

'I—feel dirty,' she whispered. 'I need a shower.'

'Right over here.' He led her to the bathroom door. 'You'll be all right by yourself? You want me to help you?'

She shook her head dumbly, stumbled over the threshold, and pulled the door shut behind her.

Undressing was difficult, but she managed it all. The shower ran cold at first. She stepped in at once. It was just what she needed to wake her up from

her daze. She let the water run cold for minutes,
lifting her face up into it, then turned on the hot
and soaped herself carefully from head to toe. Her
mind, almost comatose since the moment of the
wedding, began to function.

He needs a wife? Why? He has a perfectly good
housekeeper, and more money than he knows what
to do with, to hire others. I don't think he needs a
wife for entertainments. He has plenty of women
around, according to the newspapers. So why?
Althea? The poor little girl—perhaps she needs a
mother, but what a hard job that would be,
mothering the prickly pear. There's nothing else, is
there? He couldn't have married me just because
—no. She shut off the water and stepped out of the
shower. A full-length mirror on the wall reflected a
dripping shape, hair soaked into strands, a tired
face, drooping shoulders. He couldn't have married
me for that, she told herself fiercely—unless he's
hard up? But a man of his reputation wouldn't find
women hard to come by. Why?

The question still bothered her as she towelled
herself dry, wrapped herself in a huge bath towel,
and went out into the bedroom. Richard was already
in the bed—or rather on top of it, dressed in nothing.
Beth stopped a few feet away and studied him. It
was the first adult male body she had ever seen
naked. She studied him, from the top of his wavy
black hair to that strong neck, and muscled chest.
A narrow waist and narrow hips—and—God!—she
pulled her eyes away. No matter what he said, he
wanted her. She shuddered, and looked around the
room quickly as if an escape door might appear.

But there was no escape. Not here, not anywhere.
Pumping up her courage, she dropped her towel to
the floor and stood there. She could hear the hiss as
he drew breath quickly. Before her courage could

collapse entirely Beth walked over to the bed and sprawled herself out flat on her back, eyes on the ceiling.

'All right,' she sighed. 'Get it over with.'

'What the hell!' He rolled over closer, so her left arm rested against the warmth of his chest. She shivered at the contact. 'What did you say?'

'I said, let's get it over with,' she repeated. She was frightened half to death, but meant not to show it. Her voice was flat, emotionless. He made not a move.

'Aren't I doing it right?' she queried.

'Beth, what are you *doing*?'

'Whatever it is you need,' she sighed. 'I don't have a great deal of experience.'

'I can't believe that,' he grated. 'You and Mac, and all those nights you've spent together. I don't go for that maiden aunt business, you know.'

'I see.' She turned her head to look at him, then snapped back. It was much easier to concentrate on the ceiling. 'Funny you should say that,' she sighed. 'I couldn't sleep last night, so I got up and went downstairs to MAC. Just this morning that was.'

His hands came down on her shoulders like talons. He shook her until her head ached. 'Don't you ever tell me that again!' he grated. 'From now on I expect you to remember you're my wife. I don't want you to ever see or speak to this Mac again.'

'Please,' she said coldly, 'don't do that. My head aches, and I'm cold. Do what you want to and then leave me alone.'

'You heard what I said about your precious Mac?'

'I heard you.'

'And?'

'And I intend to do just as I please, Mr Macomber. You forced me into this marriage. If it isn't to your liking you can always divorce me.'

'Damn you!' he exclaimed. 'Damn you!'

'I probably am, anyway,' she muttered. 'I've told so many lies lately that I—I don't know. Go ahead. Rape me.'

'That's what you'd like, is it? Rape, so you'd have one *more* thing to blame me for?'

'I—I just want to get some sleep,' she muttered. 'And I can't if I'm for ever expecting you to pounce on me.'

'Well, it won't be rape, I promise you,' he said softly. One of his hands tiptoed across her stomach, while the other went behind her head, pulling her in his direction. His lips closed on hers just as his hand reached the peak of her breast. Keep cool, she told herself. Don't let him turn you on. Don't fight—just keep cool. Women don't have to be slaves to their sex drives.

His grip tightened. His first caress fled, and became an arrogant demand, pressing her back against his hand and his pillow. She struggled with all her capacity to keep calm. His hand slid off the slope of her breast and plunged down across her stomach, her thighs, into the sensitive centre of her femininity. But she held on. It was hard, but she held on. Not a move of her rigid body did she allow. Not a response to his lips or his hands. All fuelled by the growing hatred in her heart. It seemed like for ever before he got the message. She was almost at the brink of the chasm when his hand stopped, his lips withdrew, and he flung himself down flat on his back next to her, with his hands clasped behind his head.

'What the hell have I done?' he murmured.

There was no way she could answer him. All her emotions were running riot, and she could barely control herself, barely keep herself from begging him to continue. It took minutes for her to settle. He lay there rigidly for a time, then threw himself off the bed and stomped into the bathroom. She could hear the water running for a long time.

If only he had loved me, she thought vaguely. If only he had loved me. The thought pursued her as she slipped over the edge of sleep. She didn't hear him come back. He walked over to the foot of the bed and studied her while she slept. Then he carefully pulled a blanket up over her, and went out to the living-room, and his bottle of Jim Bean.

CHAPTER TEN

IT WAS the bed shaking that woke Beth up. She blinked, trying to recall where she was. It had been afternoon when she went to sleep. Now the sun was shining in the east windows, off the bay, signalling morning. Althea sat at the foot of the bed, a bouncy, smiling Althea.

'You have to wake up for breakfast, Miss Beth. Uncle Rich says you gotta—you have to—get up and go with him. Is it nice being married?'

'I—don't really know, dear. I—haven't worked at it enough. And I don't know a great deal about men.'

The girl bounced her way towards the head of the bed. Lord knows, there's plenty of room, Beth told herself. And no indication on the other side of the king-sized bed that *he* had ever been there. So he doesn't *want* me, and that leaves only one alternative. He wanted a mother for Althea.

It took a little doing, but she managed a smile for the child. 'I could help,' the child laughed. 'Uncle Rich is a softy. All you have to do is duck when he roars, and pay it no mind at all.'

'That's all, huh?' Beth struggled to sit up, pushing the covers back.

'You don't have a nightgown?'

Beth looked down at herself, startled, and pulled the blankets back up. 'No, I guess I don't,' she said wryly. 'I own one—maybe two, for that matter, but I didn't bring them with me.'

'Don't worry,' the child teased. 'Uncle has plenty

of money, he can afford to buy you anything you want. When's the next game?'

'Aha! That's your interest? We play Friday night, as usual.'

'Oh, that's not the only reason. I like you, Miss Beth. I didn't think I would, but I do. You know, when I first met you I thought you were another one of Uncle Rich's push-overs. But you sure aren't, are you?'

'How do you figure that?'

'Well, you're the only one he ever married. Are you going to have babies?'

'I—we haven't talked about that,' Beth sighed. 'I've got to find out where my clothes went. I just don't remember.'

'Must have been an exciting night,' Althea giggled. 'Your stuff is on the chair. Mrs Moore did an early wash. You'd better hurry, my uncle doesn't like to wait for people. Say, that makes you my aunt now, doesn't it?'

'I guess it does, dear. Why don't you scoot out and keep him from blowing his stack? I'll dress and be along in a jiffy.' The child scrambled for a kiss and darted out of the room, taking all the cheerfulness out of the room with her.

Beth dressed slowly, not waiting for a shower. I can get that at home, she told herself. Home? I suppose he expects me to live here—and give up my work—and just—just what? There were two ideas involved. Giving up the work was one. Just what was the other. 'I'm not going to give up my company,' she muttered as she struggled into her newly pressed clothing. 'I'm not. And he's going to demand that I do!'

It was something to build a rage upon. She worked at it during the time she was brushing her teeth, washing her face, combing her hair. By the time she

was ready the rage was of violent proportion. Only
occasionally did the 'just what' break through. Just
what did he think he was going to do to her? Share
her bed? Not on your life! Sweep her off her feet?
No chance. He'd soon find that she had very large,
firmly anchored feet! She tucked in her blouse,
pulled her skirt straight, checked herself over her
shoulder in the bathroom mirror, and went off to
do battle.

The Macombers were sitting in the little alcove
off the dining-room, inside the sliding-glass doors
that led out on to the balcony. It was a place of
maximum sunshine. Beth stopped a few feet away,
studying him. Rich was dressed more casually today.
An open-collar shirt, fawn trousers, with a Texas
ranch-jacket thrown over the chair behind him. All
his bandages were gone, and the scratches had healed.
The stitches on his cheek were visible, but not
dominant. He looked like a strong, virile, tired man.
He and Althea were making small talk. Beth took a
deep breath and walked over to the table. Richard
got up to hold her chair.

'Good morning,' he offered sceptically, like an
Indian chief come to discuss the latest peace treaty.

'I already said,' Althea added under his prompting.

Under the weight of her fancied injuries, Beth
struggled to keep a straight face. 'Yes,' she answered
softly, and ducked her head. Mrs Moore came in
behind her, and slipped a plate of ham and eggs in
front of her.

'I can't eat all that, Emily!' Beth protested.

'Can if you try,' the housekeeper stated. 'No use
you turning into a bag of bones. Dieting isn't for
newly marrieds. You need to build up your strength.'

'What for?' asked Althea.

'Don't ask,' her uncle interrupted. 'You're too
young to learn. Eat.'

'I got plenty of time,' the girl returned. 'How can I learn if nobody tells me anything?'

'Do me a favour,' her uncle sighed. 'Do all your learning at school for a week or two, will you? I've got problems at home.'

'I don't see why,' Althea continued, between bites. 'She's pretty, Uncle Rich. Nobody ever thought you'd marry a pretty one. And sensible, too.'

'Sensible?' He was pushing his food around on his plate. Beth joined in the same exercise, stopping only to sip at her coffee.

'Of course she's sensible. She manages a baseball team, doesn't she?'

'Yes, well, if you've finished, go brush your teeth and get your books together. Your Aunt Beth and I are going to work together, and we'll drop you off at your school.'

The child excused herself and ran for her room. Beth kept her head down. He stared at the top of it, of two minds as to how to approach the problem.

'I want you to come with me this morning,' he said, 'to undo the computer.'

'Yes,' she said flatly.

'And then what are you going to do?'

'I'm going to work at Rentasec,' she stated very firmly, marshalling all her rage and fear to block the expected denial.

'I see,' was all he said. Beth sat there on the edge of her chair, all the repressed anger waiting to boil over. He had failed her again. Not a bit of opposition. Not the tiniest bit. Perhaps if I nag him a little? she thought.

'I don't have any clothes with me. I suppose you expect me to live here?'

'I'm afraid I do, Beth.' She looked up at him, at the little smile that teased his lips, at the gleam deep in those dark eyes. Oh yes, she thought. I can go back to work all right, but he wants me in my cage every night for the 'just what'. Well, I'll rattle the bars, damn him. If only he had married me for love!

'Funny thoughts you're thinking?' he said. 'Care to tell me?'

'No.'

'I see. That's the way it's going to be?'

'Yes.'

Rich got up, scraping his chair back, and walked around to her side of the table. He picked up her right hand and brushed back the sleeve of her blouse. A huge black mark circled the arm just above the wrist. 'What's this?' he asked.

She looked down at it, not really seeing it. 'My wedding present from you,' she told him.

'Good God!'

'Yes.'

'Beth, I——'

'I don't want to talk about it,' she snapped at him. 'Just please leave me alone! I hate to be pawed!'

'I can see that,' he said gruffly. 'I'll be ready to go in fifteen minutes.'

'Yes,' she sighed. He stalked back to the bedroom, leaving her to cuddle her coffee mug in both hands, seeking solace. It was a difficult item to find. She refilled her mug twice, dabbled gently among the remnants of her eggs, and gnawed a piece of toast. When Rich and Althea came back, she wiped her lips with her napkin and went to join them.

'You don't look so good,' the child said. 'You always used to smile, Miss Beth—Aunt Beth.'

'Your aunt isn't feeling well,' Richard told her. 'We have to make allowances. Being newly married, and changing her home—that's a great deal of trouble. You know that, Althea, changing your home from Arizona to Boston.'

'Yes, but I had you to help me, Uncle Rich.'

'And so does Beth. It just takes time. Shall we go?'

'Last one in the car's a rotten egg,' Althea giggled, and ran for the elevator.

'I can't compete,' Rich complained. 'Look at that kid go!'

Beth looked, but said nothing. They travelled the rest of the way in silence.

'Good morning, boss. Miss Beth——' Sam the doorman was his cheerful best, in spite of the rising pollution count, and the dry-as-dust heat. 'The wife says thank you for the flowers, Miss Beth.'

'I hope she liked them,' she returned as Richard swept her into the lobby. As they waited by the elevator he looked down at her quizzically.

'What was that all about?'

'His wife has been in the hospital for three weeks, and they just brought her home.'

'Good lord,' he sighed, 'is there anyone in my employ that you don't know all about?'

She had the wild urge to scream 'Yes—you!' at him, but held herself back. 'It's just a habit I have,' she said. 'Do we have to use the elevator?'

'Of course we do. Why do you ask?'

'Because I've been stuck in this thing twice already, and you know what they say—"Three strikes and you're out".'

'I've had it overhauled since then,' he told her. The elevator hissed at her. Startled, she jumped in his direction, and for a moment found herself in his arms.

'In you go,' he coaxed. Beth crossed the fingers on both hands and stepped into the six-by-six box. Naturally it was on its best behaviour, wafting them up to the fourth floor with panache. 'See?' he said pompously.

I would dearly love to hit you, she told herself as

she followed in his wake up the corridor. Twice, at
least. She was still pondering the type of blow when
he led her into the executive suite. Grace was at her
desk. She spared a glance for Beth, but mustered a
big smile for Richard.

'The computer still won't work,' she reported
brightly. 'What do we do next?'

'Come into my office and take some dictation,
Grace. My wife is going to fix things.'

'Your *wife*?' The girl's face turned red, and the
shots she fired from her eyes would have killed lesser
mortals.

'Yes. I'll explain later.' He hurried the secretary
through into his inner office, winked at Beth, and
closed the door behind him. For some reason the
whole scene hurt. And I don't know why, Beth
thought. What could it be—envy or jealousy? I
haven't the right to either one, so why does it hurt
so badly? She pounded her fists on the desk in sheer
frustration, then turned to the computer terminal.
Everything was just as she had left it. All the
accounts were securely locked away, behind the new
password that Beth had invented.

She fished in her bag for the sheet of loose-leaf
paper containing the 'Unlock' instructions, and went
merrily down the list, permanently unlocking every
account. The machine responded to command.
'Something I guess *I* have to learn to do,' she
muttered to herself. As each account was released,
she could hear the heightened activity throughout
the building. She sat back with a sigh after fifteen
minutes of work, and watched the computer go
about its normal work. A moment later the telephone
rang.

'Beth? I knew it had to be you there.' Maggie
Berman was bubbling. 'It was a great vacation we
had, and I for one am ready to go back to work.

How are you and Macomber getting along?'

'I'm not sure, Maggie.' She felt like laughing and crying at the same time. 'Things are confused up here. I seem to have married him.'

'You what?' But by that time Beth had gently placed the telephone back in its cradle. Time to report in, and leave, she told herself. She stood up, straightened her hair, and walked over to the door. Without thinking, she followed the procedure used during the weeks she had been his secretary. She knocked once, opened the door, and walked in.

And stopped dead in her tracks. Richard was sitting back in his swivel-chair with a big grin on his face. Grace was standing dead in front of his desk with her skirts pulled up farther than that, giving him a good peep-show. She was wearing pink panties, with white lace along the bottom. The tableau held, and then the other two became aware of Beth's presence.

Richard was up out of his chair like a shot. 'She wanted to show me her operation,' he stuttered. A deadly calm came over Beth, insulating her from all the world.

'I'm sure she did,' she returned coldly. 'Check around, she may have a lot more scars to show you.' With that she turned round and walked out, closing the office door behind her. Three minutes later Grace came boiling out of the door, her face as red as a beet. The secretary stopped long enough to snatch her bag from out of her desk drawer, and went off. Richard followed, a strange look on his face.

'Beth, I want to tell——'

'Don't bother, Mr Macomber, I have no reason to know. I just wanted to tell you that your computer is unlocked. All of it. And now I would like to go.'

'Take the limousine,' he offered.

'I'll be gone the whole day. I have a lot of work

to do. Or rather MAC has a lot of work to do, and I'm going to help him.'

'Beth, don't do that to me!' His face was turning almost as red as his secretary's, and there were signs of threat in his eyes.

'I'll do anything I want to,' she returned firmly. Her legs were shivering, but she had no intention of letting him see her weakness. 'I'm your wife, not your slave.'

'Beth, I won't *let* you do this. Work all you want, but keep away from Mac!'

'You don't have the right to tell me that!' she spat. His face turned from red to puce as he took a couple of steps in her direction. Beth threw up her hands in front of her, and flinched away from him. He froze.

'Good God, Beth, you don't think I'd *hit* you? I'll never hurt you.'

'You mean no more than you already have?' she asked. His fists formed at his sides. She could see the muscles in his arms shake as he fought for control. Oh no, you won't hit me. Not today, you mean!

'I think you'd better go,' he said through clenched teeth. 'Be back here to pick me up by four-thirty.'

She nodded, swinging her golden hair around her frightened face, and ran. Out of the corridor, down the stairs, and out into the lobby. The limousine was waiting at the kerb. She climbed in as if all the devils in hell were waiting for her, and gave the chauffeur her address.

Half an hour later, with two more cups of coffee in her, and three of Mary's biscuits, life came back to normal proportions. 'And that's all you're going to tell us?' Mary asked. 'You went over to the courthouse and you married this fellow?'

'That's about all there seems to be to tell,' Beth

said wearily. 'And now, if somebody around here doesn't shut up and get to work, we'll all go bankrupt.'

Which was enough warning to stir things up. Machines pounded, telephones rang, computer terminals blinked—in short, everything was as it ought to be. Except for Beth. She went over to the corner where Rona was at work on Richard's novel, and offered to change places with her. The rest of the day she spent in second-hand contact, listening to his voice roll out the plot, while her fingers almost unconsciously repeated the words into the word-processor keyboard. It was second best, but better than nothing.

As directed, she waited outside his building at four-thirty. He came out late, puffing. 'I didn't know you were waiting,' he said, as if it were all Beth's fault. 'It's hell to be without a secretary.'

'Quit, did she?'

'Hell, no! I fired her. What a stupid stunt that was.'

'I really don't want to hear about it,' commented Beth, turning her attention to the traffic going by. He crawled into the car, cursing under his breath. She could not ever remember hearing so many four and five letter words before.

Althea was home before them, running to the door as they came in. 'Mrs Moore,' she said, talking so rapidly her words ran together. 'She got a call from her sister—and she had to go. We don't got—we haven't got any dinner. Hi, Aunt Beth.'

'Hi, Althea. No dinner? That shouldn't be hard to repair. Let's go look in the kitchen.'

'Do you want me to come along?' Rich asked.

'I can't imagine why,' Beth returned solemnly. He muttered something under his breath and went into his study. Beth and Althea strolled out to the kitchen.

On the way, the girl filled an ear about her school
day. She and the Principal didn't get along, she
didn't understand earth sciences, she wanted to be a
writer like Uncle Richard, and—the nub of it all—it
certainly was nice to have someone to talk to. Girl-
talk, that is.

Beth was a good listener, and she could feel the
need behind the words. Her hands were busy sorting
out a meal as she listened. The story went on as
Althea shredded the lettuce for a salad, and Beth
put a boneless turkey roll into the microwave. In
the middle of the discussion it struck her. The poor
child is homesick! Every other word is about her
home in Arizona, the poor dear. She lived on a
ranch, and her uncle has her imprisoned in a high-
rise. No wonder she has so much rebellion in her!

'And so could you come, Aunt Beth?'

'I missed that, dear. Could I come where?'

'To my school tomorrow. It's the last week of the
semester. Everyone else is having a parent come.
We're displaying all our art work, and stuff like that.
But Uncle Richard never comes. Would you?'

She's crying for support, Beth thought, that's all.
Just support. 'Of course I'll come, love. But
remember, we have a baseball game tomorrow night,
too.'

'Oh, there's plenty of time for all that. The exhibit
is early, ten o'clock in the auditorium, and it's
finished by noon, and we all get the rest of the day
off.'

When the meal finally came to the table Richard
joined them in his shirt-sleeves, looking a little the
worse for wear. 'I brought work home,' he said.

'Yes, I can smell it,' Beth said mildly. Althea
provided all the conversation. Beth nodded, smiled,
listened. Richard sat at the head of the table and
glowered at both of them. The conversation outlasted

the turkey, but died off in the middle of the dessert
—ice-cream cake.

Gradually the day wound down. The child had
homework, and a favourite TV movie, and then was
off to bed. The two adults sat in opposite corners of
the living-room, like two boxers waiting to come out
of their corners. Richard imitated a newspaper
reader; Beth had brought her knitting back with her,
and imitated a tired housewife until the clock
sounded eleven. She put the work away, and stood
up. He lowered his paper.

'Bed so soon?'

'Yes,' she said quietly. 'I had a busy day. I don't
plan to go to work tomorrow.'

'Mac was too much for you today, so you can't
see him tomorrow?'

She ignored the first part of the statement. 'I'm
going to school with Althea tomorrow,' she said.
'Parents do that sort of thing now and then.'

He dropped his paper, looking more and more
like a predator, with those hooded eyes. 'Don't
spend the rest of your life trying to get to me, Beth.
It doesn't pay.'

'I suppose you're right,' she agreed. 'I'm going to
bed.'

'Good idea. I'll come right along.'

'I—didn't mean it as an invitation,' she stuttered.

'Don't you think I knew that? You'd sooner share
your bed with a rattlesnake, wouldn't you?' She
suppressed the fear that washed over her. He had
come too close to seduction last night; what might
he achieve tonight?

'I—goodnight.' She turned quickly and raced down
the hall, hoping he hadn't seen the tears in her eyes.
She had already taken a shower before leaving
Rentasec, so she brushed her teeth, hurriedly
unpinned her hair, and slipped into the most

conservative nightgown she owned.

The bed had been turned down. She slid under the sheets, turned on her side, and moved as close to the edge as she could. Five minutes later she heard him come in. She closed her eyes, praying. He walked to her side of the bed and stood there, just looking. One or two words under his breath, and he went off to the bathroom. She heard the water running, and wondered.

If he loved me, I'd be in there with him, she thought. Under the spray, scrubbing each other, loving each other, learning each other. But he doesn't. You do, Beth Murphy, but he doesn't. Isn't that the classic trap, you stupid woman?

He was back, climbing into the other side of the bed. She had to hang on for dear life as his hundred and ninety pounds sent the mattress into convulsions that almost threw her out on the floor. It took him a minute or two to settle down.

'Beth? I know you're still awake. It's impossible to sleep when your body is rigid like that.' One of his hands touched her shoulder, pulled her over on her back. She hadn't realised he was so close. Her thigh came down so close to his that they touched. The warm challenge startled her. She could feel a tiny core of excitement building up in her. There was no barrier of anger to hold him off this night. He moved a little closer.

'Not so brave tonight?' His lips were right at her ear. Do something! her mind screamed at her. But she had no idea what she ought to do. She lay there like some hypnotised fool, while the sparks ran up and down her slender frame.

'Not going to make me an offer?' he teased. He moved again, coming up on his side so he towered over her. His lips were leading the attack. From her bare shoulder, up the curve of her neck, to the lobe of her ear, where his nibbling shocked her. A pleasant shock. An experience she had never had before. The hand came to her shoulder, and gently slipped the strap of her nightgown off, exposing one perfect breast. She shivered in anticipation. The lips came down, across her shoulder, into the declivity between her breasts, up to the exposed peak, nibbling.

'Oh, God,' she moaned, unable to prevent the writhing tumult that shook her.

'And it's not rape,' he whispered softly, and went back to his work. She struggled hard in a losing cause, hating herself for her weakness, enjoying the power that was bringing her low.

The little cry was too faint to be anything important, but it repeated itself, mounting until it became a scream. Beth snapped back, struggling to break free of him. 'Not now,' he muttered. 'Dear God, not now.'

'It's Althea!' she shrilled at him. The name won her release. She was up out of bed like a frightened rabbit, running down the hall. The little girl was sitting up in her bed, tears running down her face, moaning.

'It's all right, love,' crooned Beth, climbing up into the bed beside her. 'It's all right. Aunt Beth is here.' Her arm went around the child gently. 'It's only a dream, Althea. Are you awake now?'

'I—yes,' the child moaned. 'It was about Mama. I—it was terrible, Aunt Beth. Terrible!'

'More than likely it was those three helpings of turkey,' said Rich from the door. Beth threw him a glare that could kill.

'Get out of here,' she commanded. 'Can't you see the poor child has had a nightmare?'

'Can't you see the poor child needs something to settle her stomach?' he returned.

'I don't know why you're such a heartless soul,' Beth told him angrily.

'It's because I've lived with this child for a long time,' he returned. 'But if you feel like playing Joan of Arc, I can't stop you.'

'And that's the truth,' she muttered under her breath. He walked away. She cuddled the girl, who was lying at her breast, quietly crying.

The episode lasted for another ten minutes before the tears stopped. 'My stomach hurts,' the girl complained. Oh my God, Beth thought. Could that inhuman monster be right? Just in case, she scooted quietly down to the bathroom and came back with a bottle of antacid medicine. The child accepted a spoonful, and stretched out in her bed.

'Don't leave me, Aunt Beth?'

It was the kindest word that Beth had heard all day. 'No, I won't,' she whispered, and climbed into bed with her.

CHAPTER ELEVEN

FRIDAY afternoon, late. The inversion over Boston was beginning to break up. Small winds scuffled across the baseball field, raising tiny spirals of dust. Most of the boys had gone. There was a freshness to the air, and a threat of storms to come. Beth stood in the middle of the field, on the pitcher's mound, with the game ball in her hand, enjoying a moment of happiness. Her hair, made up in two small pigtails, peeked out of the back of her baseball cap, the long peak shielding her face from more freckles. Her old grey blouse was sprinkled with dirt, and her worn jeans had more patches than original cloth. She was so engrossed with her gift that she didn't hear him as he came out to her.

'Beth?' She looked up in surprise.

'Richard.' Recognition, dignity, affection, all there in one word. 'Look what the boys gave me.' She held up the little statuette, with the inscribed plate on its base. 'Look what it says, *Beth Murphy, The World's Greatest Manager.*'

'Surprised you, didn't they?'

'Lord, yes. Everything's surprised me. We hadn't won a game all season, and all of a sudden we won seven in a row. That's going out in style!'

'You've earned it, Beth. You can't earn the winning without suffering through the losing.'

She hugged the trophy to her, remembering the scene just half an hour ago. The final winning run had come across home-plate, the fans had gone berserk, and all the boys had come running out, pushed her to the middle of the field, and made the public presentation amid rounds of applause. So wonderful.

'*I* didn't earn it,' she returned thoughtfully. 'The boys did. And you. We couldn't have done it without your help. You contributed so much—including Althea. Do you think she might want to play again next year?' The last sentence came out a little wistfully. She stared up at him. Such a nice face he had. Only the scar remained on his cheek. The stitches were gone. Forceful, charming—she sighed and waited for an answer.

'No, I don't think Althea will be back next summer, Beth. Her parents will be home in three days, and she'll be going back home.'

'*Her parents? Going back home?* I—thought she was an orphan,' she queried. 'I remember very vividly your saying that her parents had gone!'

'My, how we jump at assumptions,' he chuckled. 'You've been labouring under a lot of errors, Miss Beth. Althea and Roddy are the children of my brother and his wife. Matt is an oil engineer. He took a six-month contract to inspect the workings in some Gulf sheikdom. And Kay, his wife, decided she would go with him. A second honeymoon, so to speak. So let's dump the kids off on good old Uncle Richard. They've done it before. The kids and I are old friends. That's what I meant when I said they had gone—to Arabia.'

'But—I thought——' I thought you married me because Althea needed a mother. Good lord, if not that, what?

She decided to risk it all on one question. 'Richard, *why* did you marry me?'

'Honestly?'

She nodded, a perplexed look on her face.

'It doesn't make good telling, Beth. I fell in love

with you that second morning in the office. With your cute little face, and your marvellous figure, and the firm way you ran things, and—lord, with everything about you. Including those two freckles on your nose. And then, bang, you announce wedding bells and June weddings and Mac. God, how I hate that name! When the chance came to steal you away from him, I just had to take it.'

She stared at him. She hadn't heard much beyond 'I fell in love with you.' The rest was gradually sinking into her brain. 'But I——'

He held up his hand. 'No, don't answer now, Beth. I know it was a rotten thing to do, compelling you to marriage when you were so obviously in love with another man. And breaking up your wedding plans that way—I felt like a heel. But, you know, even up to yesterday I thought I could make you return my love. Now I know better. So—I've instructed my lawyers to file for an annulment in your name. It shouldn't take long. And then you can marry your Mac. I'm more sorry than I can say. But please believe me, Beth, I never wanted to hurt you—only to love you.'

She stood as tall as she could, shoulders back, a tiny smile on her face. He loves me? I can hardly believe it! But I *want* to. How wonderful it would be, if true. What a mess I've made of everything. I wonder if it's too late?

He watched with his hands in his pockets, sorrow written in his posture, his face, especially his eyes. Her mind made up to try, she moved through the inches that separated them, threw her arms around his neck, and kissed him.

For a moment she was doing it all. Then his hands came out of his pockets and enveloped her. His lips assumed command. Their passions met at mouth, at chest, at thighs, as the whole world disappeared, leaving them alone in a tiny circle of feeling. The kiss endured until she ached for breath. A few fans straggling out of the park stopped to applaud. One particularly loud voice yelled, 'Atta boy, Macomber!' He released her, setting her back down on her feet, but still holding her loosely.

'What was that for, Beth? Goodbye?'

'Not exactly,' she responded. 'More like hello. Where's Althea?'

'I had the chauffeur take her over to her grand-mother's for the weekend. I thought perhaps I wouldn't be suitable company for her. I drove over in my Sprite.'

'Good.' She took his arm and turned him around. 'Let's go. Carry my trophy, please. And don't forget to remind me to get the surname on the plaque changed. My, you have a lot of cars—how in the devil do you get in?'

'It's pretty old,' he agreed. 'Both doors are stuck, but it goes like the wind. You have to climb over—oh, what the hell.' He picked her up, lifted her over the top of the racy little convertible, and dropped her into the bucket seat.

'Where to?' he asked as he vaulted in over the other side. Beth gave him her address, and a direc-tion or two. She took off her cap, pulled the elastic from her braids, and let the wind comb her red-gold hair.

'Magnificent,' he commented.

'Keep your eyes on the road,' she returned primly. 'We don't allow blind driving in South Boston. That big brown house on the right, see it?'

'Yes. Mac's place?'

'Not exactly,' she corrected. 'Mac lives there, but it's *my* house. Go in the driveway.' The car squealed to a stop.

'I—don't think I want to come in,' he said hesitantly. 'I'd rather——'

'Just for once, do it my way,' she said firmly. 'It won't hurt.'

'You sound like my mother,' he muttered. 'OK, I'm game. Lead on.'

She had to use her key to unlock the downstairs apartment. Mary had gone home long since, and the Rentasec offices were shrouded in canvas covers and pulled curtains. 'This is my office,' she said proudly, 'and I have to show you something.' She pulled back two of the curtains and turned on the fluorescent lights. 'Over here, please.'

The Rentasec computer was shut down for the weekend. Beth pulled its covers off, and patted the crackle-steel case. 'There he is,' she said.

'There who is?'

'That's MAC—my Multiple Access Computer!'

'What?' A roar, half-way between anger and surprise. 'A damn machine? What are you giving me, Beth?'

'Everything you want,' she returned quietly. 'Anything you want.'

'But you told me—you were living with a man, and you were going to get married in June!'

'No, Richard, I didn't. That's what *you* told *me*. All I ever did was to let you go on thinking what you already thought.'

He pulled her roughly into his arms. She leaned back from the waist and smiled up at him. 'MAC,' he muttered. 'All that time, MAC. I thought I'd eat my gut out before the week was out. You——' A thought struck him. She could see it flash across his face. 'Come on,' he ordered.

'Come on where? I have a nice big flat upstairs, and I live by myself.'

'There's something important I have to give you,'

he said firmly. 'Come on.' He left nothing to chance, but took her hand and pulled her out on to the porch.

'I have to lock up,' she gasped. 'I've got fifty thousand dollars' worth of equipment in there!' Richard allowed her the time to turn the key, and not a minute more. Back in the Sprite, he revved the engine like some Grand Tour driver, and gunned it out into the street.

'I'll come twice a week!' Beth yelled at him as they zoomed across the Congress Street bridge and turned on to Atlantic Avenue.

'What? Come where?'

'To the jail to visit you. They only allow visitors twice a week.'

'What are you talking about?'

'There's always a motorcycle cop at the next corner. At this speed, they'll lock you up and throw the key away!'

He flashed her a grin, but his foot let up on the accelerator.

'Better?'

'Safer,' she shouted back. 'I don't want to cut our friendship short.'

He scowled at that as he whipped the car up to the kerb in front of the publishing house, paying no attention to the No Parking signs. But then, she thought, who does in Boston?

'I didn't intend to be your *friend*,' he said glumly, as he hauled her out of the seat and stood her up on the sidewalk. 'Well, not *only* your friend.'

'Whatever do you mean, Mr Macomber?'

'As soon as I can find a place for it, I'll show you, Mrs Macomber.'

'Promises, promises,' she teased. He struggled with the lock on the front door. The building was totally empty, totally silent. But the elevator responded to

his signal, hissing open with aplomb. 'I'd—maybe
we should use the stairs,' she suggested humbly.

'Why in the world should we walk?'

'I don't have a good track record with your
elevator, if you remember.'

'Nonsense, woman. I've had it completely
overhauled. Step in, and let's have no more nonsense
about it.'

'Yes, sir.' Beth tipped two fingers to her forehead,
and allowed him to usher her inside. He looked so
lordly that her heart ached. *And he loves me. And I
love him!* The elevator gave her an ugly hiss, shook
itself a couple of times, and started upward.

'We've got a great deal of talking to do,' he said.
There was possession and passion and domination
all wrapped up in his words.

'We're going to have time to talk?' she asked
anxiously. The elevator must have heard. It thumped
a couple of times, and came to a dead stop half-way
between the third and fourth floors.

'Oh, my!' groaned Beth. She swallowed the impulse
to say, I told you so. The man she loved was looking
down at her with a pained expression on his face. It
seemed, to an inexperienced wife, a good time to
shut up or whistle, and her throat was too dry for
whistling.

Richard worked over the box of buttons a time
or two, pounding rather than pushing. The old
elevator groaned, but refused to move. From the
back of him, she thought sure he was in a rage. His
shoulders shook, and he pounded one big fist on the
steel wall.

'I told you the elevator had a grudge against me,'
she offered.

'It's not your fault.' He turned around, grinning.
Beth gave a big sigh of relief. 'What's that mean?'
he asked suspiciously.

'Well,' she said honestly, 'it means here I am trapped in a little cubicle with a man I hardly know anything about——'

'Except that he loves you,' he interrupted.

'Well, yes—there's that. I'm glad you're laughing. I thought—it isn't important. Do you think they'll rescue us pretty soon?'

'Don't dodge the issue,' he said seriously. 'You thought I was in a flaming rage, and you were afraid. Don't be, Beth. Ever. Yes, I go through the roof at times. All Macombers have bad tempers. But I'll never hurt you, love. Never.'

'I—I'm glad,' she sighed. 'It's—so hard to know. I grew up with a father and four brothers, and thought I knew everything there is to know about men. But it's different being married to one. It's like turning all your heart and life into someone else's keeping. I guess what I'm saying is it takes a lot of trust.'

'And do you trust me?'

'Yes. Very much so.' She rubbed the tip of her itching nose and grinned back at him. 'Now, when are they going to come and rescue us?'

'Who? The building's empty. Nobody knows we're here. The next caller will arrive around midnight. That's the security team that checks once a night.'

'Oh, my! We'll be here until midnight?'

'Just about. If we're lucky, that is.'

'Oh, my!' she repeated.

'You say that a lot, don't you?'

'I—only when I'm nervous. Is it a Federal crime?' He shrugged his shoulders and sat down on the carpet.

'Might as well make ourselves comfortable,' he suggested. It sounded more like an order than a suggestion to Beth. She moved a few feet away from him and sat down, too. Silence prevailed. It became so quiet that she could hear the quakes and quivers of the old building as it settled for the night. So what do we do now? Count our fingers? she thought. Is there a deck of cards in your bag?

'I've got some chewing gum,' she offered. 'I carry it for the boys. It relaxes them when they're playing.' And why am I babbling, for goodness' sake? I'm trapped in an elevator for six hours or more with my husband. The instant thought that followed brought the blood rushing to her cheeks. He reached out a hand for a stick of gum, without saying a word.

Five minutes seemed like five hours. Beth stirred restlessly and glanced over at him, to find him devouring her with his eyes. She needed something to say. 'Why did we come over here, anyway?'

'I have two things in my desk I wanted to give you,' he said solemnly.

'And you're not going to tell me what?' Don't look at him, she schooled herself. It's the only way to survive!

'I'd be glad to tell you. There's a tape, with something about blackmail on it. And then there's a wedding contract. I wanted you to have them both, so you would know I was keeping nothing to hold over your head. I thought, back there at your office, that I might give it one more try. To get you to love me, that is. But you—I don't know. I'd expected a knock-down fight with you, but there doesn't seem to be a struggle.'

'That's pretty big of you, after telling me you would get our marriage annulled, and I could go to MAC.'

'Your MAC is very lucky he's a machine, lady.'

'Why?' she asked.

'Because when I went into that house I was fully prepared to beat him to death, throw you over my shoulder, and take you away with me.'

Beth shifted nervously a few inches farther away from him. 'But—you said, at the ball park——'

'I was a fool at the ball park. I came to my senses in that drive to your house. You're my woman—and I mean to keep you! Do you have anything to say about that?'

'I—no. Only there was that little incident with your secretary. Perhaps you'd like to say something about that?'

He seemed to be having trouble getting started. 'I had nothing to do with it, Beth. Honestly.' His eyes did a quick scan of her face. She did her best to maintain a neutral front, but hiding the laughter was difficult. 'Well, I didn't,' he repeated with injured innocence. 'She just walked in and said I should look at the result of her operation, and up went the skirt. And that's all!'

'But you didn't mind looking. I seem to remember you were thoroughly enjoying it.'

'OK, so I was enjoying it. But damn it, woman, I didn't instigate it. You have to believe me.'

'Oh, I believe you,' she chuckled.

'Why, you little witch! You were playing me along, weren't you? Come over here!' She slid a few inches in his direction. 'More than that. *Way* over here.' She moved another few inches, only to find her hand captured in his. One tug and she was in his lap.

'What—what are you doing?'

'We have six hours or more before rescue arrives, and we have to find something to do.'

'Yes?' she responded breathlessly. 'You've thought of something?'

'I have this fixation,' he chuckled. 'I keep hearing your niece saying that you're her maiden aunt. We need to do something about that.'

'I—but—I'll always be her aunt. What are you talking about?' She fell back in his arms, squinting up into his face. Those dark eyes were lit up with amused purpose. His hand worked gently at the buttons down the front of her blouse.

'You mean—right here?'

'That's why I had this nice soft carpet installed.'

'But the elevator is only six feet wide. You're six foot two!'

'Flunked geometry, did you? The square of the hypotenuse is equal to the sum of the squares of the other two sides?'

'I heard that in school once. I didn't believe it. What does it mean?'

'It means that if we were to stretch out diagonally here there would be plenty of room for fun and games.'

An hour later Beth opened her eyes to find herself lying naked beside her husband. He stirred when she did. 'Did I hurt you?' He sounded so anxious that she couldn't help smiling.

'Only a little,' she sighed happily. 'I never knew it could be so—wow! Could we——?'

'Do it again?'

'Please!'

'You say that very nicely, lovely lady. What's that big smile on your face all about?'

'I was just wondering.'

'About what?'

'I wondered if there were a category in the Guinness Book of Records for doing it in an elevator.'

'Good God, I've married a shameless hussy!'

'Well, I was going to tell our——'

'If our children hear a word about this, Beth, you're in trouble!'

'It seems to me I'm in trouble no matter which way I go. But I won't tell our children. Only our granddaughters. Why—why don't you push the Emergency button?'

'Because I've got the emergency well in hand,' he leered.

'What are you doing?'

Both his hands settled just under her breasts. 'One thing I hate is a babbling woman,' he said. His fingers began to move. No further words were required.